COUNTERINTELLIGENCE

MICHELE PACKARD

PRAISE FOR PACKARD'S BOOKS

" ... One of the things I love most about Ian Fleming's James Bond movie is the scenery and like a Bond movie Matti takes us around the world to exotic places we will never see. Ms. Packard's skill at describing these places and making them real for her readers is second to none in her profession (nothing personal Mr. Fleming).

Matti's penchant for using pop culture references not only makes her much more relatable, but it also adds a strong sense of familiarity to her story as well as having the added effect of making the reader a part of the story. Throw in the author's knowledge of current events and her skill of weaving those events into her stories makes for reading that feels like the just recently here and now.

One of the best character development series I have seen are the 'Lethal Weapon' movies and Ms Packard does not fall short of that mark. Her characters are alive with feelings, attitude and wit making the reading all the more enjoyable. Matti's depth of character reaches out and draws us in, it makes us want to be a part of Matti's adventure and her friend. Which is by now the third story where I am, liking Matti and wanting to get to know her even more.

I can in all honesty say that this is the best series of books I have read since I read 'Curse of the Clansmen and King' by Linnea Tanner. Everything about this series starting with Aesop and ending with Teller sets (for me at least) a whole new level in reading that is fast paced, thrilling and enjoyable. I can go on and on about this series and this story, but the best thing I can do is recommend that you read it for yourself, it will not disappoint." — Richard

With a review like this, what more do you really need to know?!
Richard also has a role in this book based off this review.
Just saying...you could be in the next book!

ACKNOWLEDGEMENTS

This book is dedicated to my family.
Today, Tomorrow and Always.

And to my dear friend Ashley,
who sent me my first #morematti text 🤍

To every reader who purchases:
Thank you for your support and hope you enjoy the adventures.

Carpe diem

Counterintelligence

1. Activities designed to prevent or thwart spying, intelligence gathering, and sabotage by an enemy or other foreign entity.

PRELUDE

MY HEART STOPPED...I knew what I had just witnessed. He was laughing, smiling, and telling a story with his hand waving excitedly in the air, reenacting the story. Then his right eye went murky, just like in *Mission Impossible*.

He was dead.

Even without training, you recognize death when you see it. As a specially trained operative, we are proficient in seeing the most miniscule change in a person's eyes and movements before the precipitating event that will signify when they strike or are beaten. Just like Ralphie in *A Christmas Story*, where you see him flip and finally beat up the bully. You knew the moment he flipped. The human brain can process entire images that the eye sees in milliseconds. Rapid processing speed had me flash back to the last twenty-four hours like pictures in an album. A tear rolled down my right cheek. *Why him?*

My team had been in Vail, Colorado on a scouting mission. My best friend and work counterpart Bethany, two of the best retired navy seals Jake and Steve, and Doug, here, who came to assist me with a special personal request were all with me.

Ever since the virus arrived, the world had not been the same. Millions had died worldwide, including the President and Vice President of the United States. The debates and uncertainty over succession, riots, protests, and unemployment were on the rise. "Stay at home to save Granny" was echoed loudly, but also, "Let's congregate by the hundred thousand to protest." Can't attend a sporting event or even a funeral, concerts are no longer kosher, your neighbor will call you out on Nextdoor if you aren't wearing a mask…epic meltdown. People were scared and desperate. Desperate people do desperate things.

Nine months, the US had been in isolation. The division it caused in political parties, race and even gender would last long after I would be gone and would be up for discussion for centuries to come. The economic impact would not be fully known for generations. I had been arguing this concern for decades, to no avail; but to beat our enemies, you had to be willing to do what is considered unacceptable and unthinkable.

I had a million thoughts going through my head. Another lone tear strolled down my face as John Waite's *Missing You* flashed through my thoughts…*and I'm wondering why you left, and there's a storm raging through my frozen heart tonight…*

Right now, I had to tackle a more immediate issue in front of me. We were driving 75mph on I-70, and Doug was dead behind the steering wheel.

ONE

Colorado

EVEN WITH THE BEST INTEL, the American public will never know the true course of action that has impacted their lives forever. A little virus, a submicroscopic infectious agent that invades living cells, was causing havoc across the world. I'm all too familiar with this idea, being a man-made product myself, spending my lifetime to ensure that no one in the public domain would get their hands on what created me for fear of a New World Order. All these years, I have worked to safeguard the distribution of MY virus, but there was a larger picture at play.

This new virus was smart. You had to admire its tenacity and ability to mutate. It selectively took its victims with no logic. At first, it was believed to target those with compromised immune systems and the elderly. But that changed as it proceeded to attack the healthy, as well, with no method or discrimination.

China, of course, was blamed for the spread, and you saw efforts to shield their participation. Was it honor or self-preservation? Of course, other countries, including ours, assisted in the cover-up, which begged the question, what were the true motives, and who were the responsible parties? Most importantly, what was the end game?

The world went on lockdown for the first time since WWII, with technology allowing everyone to see, heightening tensions and misdirecting attention. Economies were obliterated as governments mandated the shutdown of restaurants, non-essential businesses, churches, and educational systems; all in futile attempts to contain the virus. The virus just laughed and spread more.

Group gatherings were not permitted. Families mourned privately upon the death of a loved one. Elementary school kids were learning over Zoom while their parents also juggled work from home. Masks and anti-bacterial products soared, and people became creative. Zoom calls went viral overnight while we watched in horror as cities, government buildings, and historic statues were torn down by extremists. Unlike 9/11, we were a house divided…with no end in sight.

And there was more than just a deadly virus. The United States was experiencing unprecedented fires, hurricanes, and even murder hornets. Skeptics were calling it the "year of the apocalypse." Scary times—and unlike history, technology elevated evil. The respected boundaries of civility went out the window, and professional courtesy was no longer needed or warranted. You need eyes in the back of your head. Reminds me of *American President*: *"How do you have patience for people who claim they love America, but clearly can't stand Americans?"*

I'm pretty confident that 'fearporn' has now been added to Webster's (or, if not, it will be). "Keyboard warriors" are what I call them, playing off anonymity, misdirecting, and hiding behind the screen, but coming after others with a vengeance.

As a private government contractor working secretly and directly under the authority of the President of the United States, I was in a precarious position. My last assignment was to investigate and report back to the President on the FDA and the US's growing dependence on China for pharmaceutical drugs. China accounts for seventy percent of the market. The FDA had been ordered to expand regulation and inspection. Looks like we were a little too late, here, as the President and Vice-President were no longer with us.

Thus, my predicament. No one knew I was secretly working directly on assignment for the highest-ranking elected official. I could trust no one...not that I ever had.

There were disturbing trends that no one was seeing, that could be used for misdirection. Since the virus, social networking soared as the public looked for any new information. YouTube saw a huge increases worldwide. YouTube is a Google company. Google is owned by Alphabet, Inc. Google China is the largest search engine in the world. Zoom was founded by a Chinese-American billionaire. TikTok, owned by ByteDance, a Chinese company, was being forced to relinquish control to US companies due to concerns over intellectual rights and the compilation of consumer insights. The number one gaming company, Roblox, is owned by Tencent, which is forty-nine percent owned by Chinese. Pharmaceutical companies manufacturing vaccines at an unprecedented rate had large ties to...China.

Why were free-thinking Americans not seeing this disturbing trend? Because we are no longer "free." Who is censoring and (mis) directing the general public to only what they want them to see...for profit? Media.

You and I can both search the same thing on our browsers and receive different results. Computer-generated algorithms determine that the next piece of information that you see based on predictability and more importantly, profitability. It is no longer the news telling you *when* to think about something, but it now tells you how to think, and only shows you what they want you to see. There can be no unity until this is rectified. It's a new evolution, and the public is being willingly played, and is losing.

I call it the "rose-tinted glasses effect." John Conlee wrote about it in his song…*But these rose-colored glasses, that I'm looking through, show only the beauty, 'cause they hide all the truth…*

Everyone is wearing them. You see only what 'they' want you to see or are directed to see. When faced with reality, it's your mind/body's reaction to protect itself with an optimistic perception of something—a positive opinion or a 'like' on social media. It's thinking something is better than what it is. In this age of technology, it's willed ignorance. Our greatest sin.

During this new virus age, social sharing networking skyrocketed. Not just Facebook and Instagram, but Twitter soared, and messaging apps like WhatsApp and Skype, with Cloud storage, was the industry that profited during this chaos. It's a Twitter world, not a real world.

The continued debate over the dissemination of (mis) information over who generated, created, and released this virus, was epic. Finger pointing was done by all countries. America and China were being set up for WWIII.

The US has a higher GDP for now, but China has passed us on PPP (Purchasing Power Parity). China's population has four times that of the US.

Listen, folks, it's a matter of simple math. Once China surpasses us, we can never catch up, as we play the stats forward and China is in it to WIN. They want it more. They believe it's their time, and they will stop at nothing. So, it naturally makes sense that they've created this world havoc, as they have the numbers to sustain anything. Including a little human-generated virus. They are using every part of their nation to influence us diplomatically, economically, politically, and militarily...and they are winning, at the moment. They don't need to be worried about the US; we are fighting ourselves. We are a house divided.

Wait...back up. What did I first say? ...*to beat our enemies, you have to be willing to do what is considered unacceptable, unthinkable*.... I had to think bigger: step out of the box and predict who ultimately would win this game.

I swore an oath to the United States of America and had to find out the truth at all costs and stop this. Another tear rolled down my face as I contemplated what to do. Marilyn Manson's *Killing Strangers* played on the radio...*We're killing strangers so we don't kill the ones we love...*

TWO

WHEN THE PRESIDENT DIED, my professional world went on pause. Until last year, my assignments were coordinated by Freddy (who I thought was my biological father, but, in fact, was just an outside participant in a test gone awry). Freddy had tried to assist in protecting me my whole life, albeit very unsuccessfully, at times. Not that I think I was a mistake. In fact, I was manufactured to be a "super-being," and learned I had two brothers that were considered inferior at the conclusion of the experiment. How's that for women's lib?

(Stop. I did not get to my position based on being a woman, or to fill some HR hire quota. I'm the best, as I've trained to be the best. It's insulting for me to consider otherwise. I wasn't given participation medals. I learned, from success and failures, to climb and even crawl to my success. I'm the best in my field because I will do what you won't...I'll work harder because I AM a driven elite. Ok, I digressed for a moment...)

When this virus was announced, I took precautions for my own family first. My gorgeous, loving husband, Tom, was honing his skills to better assist me on assignments, and we decided to stay in Texas for the time being. Our college-age triplets, Matthew, Mark, and Mary were continuing their specialized military training in Colorado Springs under Jake and Steve, who were designing a new program for the next generation of soldiers. We recalled (retired) Sergeant Ainsworth to stay on board during this transition, who was more than willing to collect a paycheck during these unprecedented times. Bethany had stayed back in Texas with Tom and me—with much reluctance, as she had recently started a "relationship" with Steve. *(I swear she's going to be the death of me.)* Freddy was still on the mend from our last assignment, where he and I were officially declared dead, and he was slowly recovering from being shot in the chest. So, it was a little tricky to navigate, to say the least.

Bethany still had an occasional assignment and mission, but I had to lay low until I could "re-emerge" successfully, and, unfortunately for me, the President was to assist in my resurrection. Without the President, I was also not getting paid, just like the other millions now unemployed. (Not asking for sympathy here, just making a statement.)

I organized my team to meet in Vail, Colorado for an exploratory visit, as this was the epicenter for the spread of the virus to other countries. Two flights carrying high-level Mexican dignitaries returned to their country testing positive. And, from there, it went rampant across all countries. With no contact tracing in place, there was no way to predict where it had originated or where it was headed. The world watched in horror as numbers of deaths quickly rose from thousands to millions with flu-like symptoms. The numbers continue to climb.

We had an inside informant, Richard Dominguez, who was assisting us with putting the dots together, and we needed his intel to close loops. It didn't hurt that Richard had an Antonio Banderas vibe going on. Bonus. His expertise guided us to what we had long suspected. The virus was in the US months before our government had informed the public, and before it was "supposedly" accidentally released by China.

Across the US, guess who was purchasing, at over asking price, commercial and residential properties with no inspection, no appraisals, and one hundred ten percent cash offers? Yeah, that would be China.

As commercial travel was initially restricted and businesses went on lockdown, we waited for the right openings. Being expertly proficient in disguises for my profession was now moot, as everyone had to wear masks.

Waiting around was not necessarily my forte. Some took this down time to learn and strengthen skills, while others saw it as a reprieve from everyday life. When my darling husband started watching *90-Day Fiancé*, I knew I could no longer sit idle. It was time to act. *Sweet Jesus.* I had to remind myself that we were in unprecedented times, and we were all on our own journeys.

Texas was not as strict as Colorado in terms of restrictions, but Colorado did open for the winter ski season (ka-ching…money). We were traveling privately on the Gulfstream G650ER that Bethany had previously "leased" for our team. This trip was to serve a few agendas with tracking down the host, releasing some built-up tension on the slopes, and stopping by to check on the kids on the way out. Jake and Steve, in superior athletic form, hit the double blacks and back bowls hard. Tom, an excellent skier, and athlete in his own right, was keeping up with them with no problem. Bethany and I opted for the timed runs, in fierce competition with each other. We were humbled when an adaptive skier blew past us to the finish line. We raced back to the top, and that's when *it* happened.

Others warn you all the time to be careful on your last run on the last day. Your body is tired, you're fighting elevation, dehydration, and fatigue, and that's when you make mistakes.

Bethany and I were on the lift taking us to the top of Highline for the last run to end our tiebreaker streak. I had just gotten off the lift and pivoted to see the starting line, while waiting on Bethany. We had come up on the single lift line to avoid the line. *(The false perception was that this was helping reduce the spread of the virus. Don't get me started.)*

I was doing NOTHING, but knew I had just torn my meniscus. Mother f'er. I've been rebuilt by doctors so many times, it was literally just a matter of time. But, really, now? Not when I was killing a known terrorist and protecting our country, but NOOO. It had happened just doing the everyday thing of turning around. #screwthisyear.

I said nothing. Bethany took no mercy on me on that last run, despite my best efforts. "Damn, we need to get you in better shape if I'm going to bitch slap you like that. I'll go join the boys if you continue like that," she teasingly offered after I crossed the finish line. We had known each other since "the academy," and she has been part of my family ever since. She's more than my best friend. After all we have been through, she is my blood. She also scares the bejesus out of me most of the time, so really, she is just like family, in that sense.

"It's not fair to always win, so I thought I'd allow you a small glimpse into the other side."

"Are you kidding me? I smoked your ass. I OWN you." She continued walking with an overly inflated, confident smirk.

"Shut it, woman; we all have off days. Track down the boys and head to the shot wheel while I stop at the restroom."

"I'd be shitting in my pants, too, if I skied like that," she said as she walked towards Garfinkle's patio.

Once in the restroom, I called our pal Doug to see if he could come over and join us. He was right down the road in Beaver Creek. I didn't want to tell Tom, or anyone else, yet, of my dilemma. *I know. Vanity at its best.* I was going to need to see Dr. Rihani for a check-up.

Doug was an ex-college baseball player turned Delta Force. His call sign was Golden Eagle, but technically he could have been Whore Monger. He was personable as all get out, came from family money, had an amazing memory, and was a great resource for the team to utilize, on occasion. Bonus? He was extremely loyal to me, for whatever reason. Jake and Steve had a friendly, but sometimes long, banter with Doug over which was better - Seals vs. Delta. Egos, right?

We stayed at that shot wheel much longer than any of us had intended. I felt like it landed on Jameson the whole time. The boys were bragging over their jumps, and Bethany was still reeling from her victory. We laughed and hollered and got the remaining patrons to join in the shenanigans. We all needed this reprieve. Some bad karaoke was part of it, the masks not helping our limited abilities. We headed back to The Ritz Carlton and talked about what we'd found out during our visit, and the next course of action.

Jake, Steve, and Tom wanted to head straight to Colorado Springs to check on the training facility and the kids before we all departed. Bethany wanted to sleep in, then join them, as that meant more time with Steve before we all went our separate ways. I informed the team that Doug and I had a detour to Denver International Airport to follow up on a lead before joining them, and we would leave earlier in the morning and would rendezvous with them in Colorado Springs to see the kids.

Tom and I headed to our room to do the customary tradition of sharing a bottle of Abacus before any new mission, leaving the rest of them in the lobby bar. We could hear them whooping it up all the way to the elevators.

"Matti, I have some reservations about this. You don't have the normal support that you are accustomed to…" He trailed off.

"Are you going to open that bottle and let it breathe?"

"Stop deflecting," he responded, looking at me with those penetrating blue eyes of his.

"Tom, you know how I'm wired. I can't just sit here and let this chaos continue."

"No, I understand that part. But it's just you, this time. Or, just "your" team. You don't have enough support. There are too many players. It's not your responsibility."

"It's everyone's responsibility, Tom. As individuals, we can't allow our freedoms and liberties to be taken without merit or repercussions. Look around. Civility is out the window. Our first amendment rights have been violated. There's censorship on all levels. We've opened the technological Pandora's box and it is swallowing up this nation and world as a whole. I *might not* make a difference, but I have to try. I can't wait…I won't wait in hopes that someone else, or our government, will make the right decision. I, we, don't have that luxury. I'm also part of another problem. I may not always win, but I never quit a fight."

"Did you just *Cobra Kai* a Johnny quote? Good lord, I couldn't stop you if I wanted to." He paused, then added, "And if I was a betting man, I'd put my money on you every time."

"Damn, Skippy. You trying to sweet talk me? I appreciate the sweet talk thing you got going on here, but let me give you a tip: I'm the sure thing."

"And you give me grief about my TV watching choices. You misquoted, by the way. How many times can you watch those movies from the eighties?"

"*Cobra Kai* was this year and *Pretty Woman* was in the nineties. Get your dates right and come over here…" I had my own version of *Let's Go to Bed* by the Cure, playing…*Doo doo doo doo, let's go to bed*…

THREE

I AWOKE WITH A BIT OF A HEAD THUMPER. Shots plus wine does not equate to good times. Not at my age, at least. Doug was in the lobby holding a triple shot latte for me when I arrived. Bless this man.

"Your chariot awaits," he said as he pointed to my rented black Range Rover Velar SV Autobiography Dynamic.

"Sweet ride. Where is yours?"

"I gave my keys to the G-wagon to Bethany last night."

"That one is yours?" I asked as I pointed to the valet section.

"Just remember that I'm not on a secret governmental payroll at present, so your fee may need to be reduced," I retorted, with a nagging dull ache in the back of my head.

"Oh, my rate doesn't change. I dropped what I was doing to come over here. In fact, I may charge extra."

"Killing me, Smalls. I can't handle it this early. Let's get on the road."

The I-70 pass from Vail to Denver is a winding road through the mountains, with two tunnels. The Eisenhower Memorial tunnel is the highest vehicular tunnel in the world, at over eleven thousand feet, and is the longest tunnel of the Interstate highways. If it's a hard snow, the tunnels shut down and you can see the lines for miles as passengers wait it out. Weekend traffic is terrible, as skiers/vacationers leave early to escape to the mountains.

We were in luck, with clear sunny skies and mostly dry roads. Doug was maneuvering with expert precision, but at a fast pace. I was still a bit queasy none the less. Steep grade signs adorn the roads every few miles, with runaway lanes for eighteen wheelers or cars that have brake failure.

"Hung over, still, or just being quiet, this morning? You haven't said much. Since you were vague on your request and mislead the group on 'our' true intentions about where we are headed, I assume Tom doesn't know, either, based on the convos last night."

"Your driving is not helping this head thumper, but no…I need to see our pal, Dr. Rihani."

Dr. Rihani was THE expert on rebuilding and had assisted me over the years. He specialized in plastics, but was the doc on call for the Olympic Skiing Team, who happened to practice in Vail. He really was a wiz doc, able to accommodate any request, and left no visible scars. Thus, he was the preferred doc for the discriminating superstars, with a bevy of who's who of the rich and famous. He was easy on the eyes, too. Bonus. Doug had used him recently, himself, for a tear in his shoulder.

"What did you do?"

"Think I tore my meniscus skiing. Actually, not even skiing; just turning."

"Meniscus. That's it? I busted over here to drive you for this? Hell, take two Tylenol and get over it. Why didn't you just tell Tom?"

"I know I should have. I will tell him, but just felt off, lately. I need a full check-up…not just physically…"

"Holy shit. THE Matti Baker is acknowledging that she's just like the rest of us, with all our faults and perils. You're no spring chicken anymore, huh?" he mocked.

Ouch. That was the crux of my concern(s). I can't be like everyone else. I was 'developed' not to be like everyone else. I don't know what I feared more: growing older and being mentally not there, or being physically not there. After everything I have been through, it may be just both. It was paralyzing me and crippling my thoughts. Damn, aging sucks.

Doug understood. That's why I called him. I actually needed his moral support. He was unwillingly "retired" from Delta Force after a freak accident that left him unable to perform his duties to the level that they needed.

All those years of pitching in college caught up to him, and despite the best military medical efforts, they could not repair his shoulder to a level of satisfaction, and just like that, his service was no longer needed. If only he had the option to go to Rihani sooner. No thank you, big gifts, or going away parties…just, "you are no longer needed."

Oh, Doug understood my predicament. These days, the military will release you for eczema. They can afford to be selective. Should they be, is another discussion.

"Don't panic. Let's get you to the good ol' Doc and do a thorough check-up. I'm sure you are fine, Matti. Trust me, you are the only person in my life I would drop everything for. I know you'll figure this all out and get us out of this crazy mess. In fact, I bet Doc pisses me off and tells you that you are better than ever. I could stand to get a check-up from him, too. Your treat, of course."

"You all are going to drain every last penny from me, you greedy mo-fos." *I loved this dude.* "So, how late did ya'll stay out last night?"

"Holy shit. I don't know if it's because everyone had been couped up for so long, or most likely the shots earlier, but the gang was on a big-time roll. Steve gave money to the bartenders and anyone else he could find to keep the bar open late. Bethany was on top of the bar, ordering more food and doing…I don't know what the fuck she was doing. Jake was talking to some stranger. Obviously, the alcohol taking its toll, as she was way above his pay grade, but he managed to lure the skank over to us for more shots. She bought, so no complaints. Only Jake and I were stupid enough to take more, but I was just shooting for moderation, as I knew we were leaving before everyone else. No pun intended."

"I'm not buying that; you are normally the instigator." I laughed, with a tinge of pain in the back of my skull.

"Ha ha. Oh my god, I have to tell you!" He was animated as he was about to share. "This was too funny; I can't believe I almost forgot…"

And that's when it happened. He was facing me to tell me, with a broad smile on his face, his soft brown eyes radiating with cheer, and in a blink of an eye he was gone.

One second…I had processed it all. I grabbed the wheel instinctively to maneuver, realizing I needed my body to cross over the cumbersome middle console area. Doug was 5'11, 225 lbs of solid muscle. I first attempted to pick up his dead, weighty right leg in an attempt to put on the brake. We weren't slowing. The brakes were also out. *Mother…fuckers.* Somebody wanted us dead. Big mistake. Huge.

While steering through the windy roads at this speed, I was honking and flashing lights to get cars out of my lane, swearing at these fuckwads who wouldn't get out of the way. What happened to the days when you could flash your lights and people knew to move the fuck over?! I tried to move the seat back to get on top or in front of Doug, but there simply wasn't enough room in this luxury vehicle. I hit the emergency parking brake in the middle console and was preparing for a spin on this mountain range with no guardrail…and nothing.

Think. Outside of trying to open the ninety-pound door over the weight of a 225 lb. male at seventy-five miles per hour and attempting to push poor Doug out on the open highway, my options were getting smaller and smaller.

I wasn't jumping, either. I already had a messed-up knee. Where are those damn runaway lanes when you need them?! Why can't I do simple math right now?!

Just then, Bethany called, and I hit answer almost screaming. "B, tell me some good news, and tell me you have left," I said, exasperated, as I was about to careen with the idiot in front of me who wouldn't get out of the way as I contemplated shooting him with my Glock.

"I'm coming up on you. I couldn't sleep. DYING from last night, so just got on the road and noticed your GPS."

"Haul ass, chica… I'm in a dilemma. Car has no brakes and no driver. I need a plan B."

"What the fuck! I'm less than a mile behind."

One mile equals sixty seconds at a sixty-mile pace. Bethany wouldn't be going sixty in the G-wagon, so I estimated I had less than forty seconds to continue maneuvering through the now-crowded lanes.

I attempted to slow myself on the small banks, but that just slowed down the drivers even more. Worst case, I hit the idiot in front of me to slow me down. But I had no control over how they would react. In fact, it could end up worse. If I used the concrete medium to slow me down, I could end up flipping with the traffic behind me and causing even more damage and deaths.

Drivers were visibly cursing me, unaware that I was about to cause their demise, as well, if I didn't get this under control. We had just passed Silverthorne where it opens to three lanes, but I had the Eisenhower/Johnson tunnel coming up quickly.

Come on, Bethany, hurry the hell up.

I looked at Doug, who was no longer Doug. His eyes were lifeless and still open. *I'm so sorry, Doug. This is my fault. I'm so sorry.* Another tear. *Stop it, not now. GD hormones!*

B was coming up fast and furious. She was making Vin Diesel look like a pussy. When you're driving a G wagon at one hundred and ten miles per hour, people instinctively get out of the way when they see it in their rearview window.

Damn you, Range Rover. She was passing on the passenger side and looked at me while I was still steering over Doug's lifeless body.

"Getting in position. You know what to do."

"On my count….3-2-1…"

The Range Rover hit her bumper harder than what I preferred while she expertly slowed us down over the next miles. Smoke was coming from her car as we descended the mountain pass, and she used the weight of her car to slow mine down. At this point, people finally caught a damn clue and were getting out of our way, while taking pictures. Idiots.

Finally (what felt like forever), she had us at a stop and we were able to pull away from the traffic just before we hit the tunnel. She got out of her car and walked over to Doug's side as I rolled down the window.

She stared at him, shaking her head vehemently. "God dammit!"

"B, we don't have time right now. Where are the boys? If Doug was targeted, they most likely were, too!"

"Jake and Tom were heading out probably fifteen minutes after me. Steve was still sleeping after passing out last night."

I dialed Tom immediately. "TOM! Are you driving? Where are you?! Am I on speaker?"

"Not too far from you. Jake was driving, but we're pulled over for gas. He can hear you. Why? What's up, love?"

"Jake, listen to me. Grab the med kit *now*! Tom, listen carefully and do exactly what I tell you. I'll walk you through what you need to do for Jake."

For the next sixty seconds, I instructed Tom what to do on Jake to dislodge a micro-explosive capsule from his head. My thoughts were racing, and Bethany was looking just as scared as I was. I instructed Tom methodically on what to do, silently praying.

Please God, PLEASE God, don't take Jake, too.
"Tom? Jake?
Nothing.
"JAKE?"
"I'm...still here," responded Jake in a trembling voice.

Bethany and I looked at each other, relieved, the color draining and returning to our face, our white knuckles loosening.

"What the hell, Matti? Who? How?! More importantly, why?" she begged to me in a whispered tone.

"It looks like my resurrection is coming to fruition sooner than I expected," I solemnly reflected.

"Whatcha going to do?" she asked. Which was more of a statement than a question.

Yeah, fuck the *Bad Boys* remake. Have they not been watching the news? *Bad Girls, Bad Girls...*

Plus, I was still reminiscing on Doug, and had the slower tune of Boston's *More than A Feeling...So many people have come and gone, their faces fade as the years go by, yet I still recall as I wander on, as clear as the sun in the summer sky...*

FOUR

I WAS GOING TO HAVE TO HOLD OFF on Dr. Rihani, as I had bigger issues to tend to versus a torn meniscus and a hormonal psyche. Bethany and I loaded Doug into the G-wagon and detoured to Colorado Springs to meet up with the boys after they rectified their own brake issue. We didn't talk during the drive, but felt the weight and magnitude of the situation in front of us.

Ainsworth met us in front of the facility to assist in the arrangements with Doug while we went inside to meet up with the team and kids. The kids were in different PT intervals, and I watched as they ran, bear crawled, and hit the assault bike in their respective timed areas. They had no idea what we had just been through, nor would they ever. There were twenty in this class, and my kids were kicking ass and taking names, compared to the rest of them. Pussies. Proud mommy moment, despite the present circumstances.

Mark saw me first. "Mom!"

Matthew and Mary turned around and all three came towards me, not sure if they were more excited about the temporary reprieve in their workout or just generally happy to see me. I told myself it was the latter and hugged them as if it had been years versus months.

"We didn't think you would be here. Or, that you'd be later. We just started. We need to see if Ainsworth will let us resume later," Matthew indicated.

"No, no. Continue on. Ainsworth is in an important meeting right now. I need to meet with the team to discuss some issues, anyways, and then we can spend some time before we must head out again. Ainsworth is going to be tied up for a bit, so just carry on."

"Mom, we can do this later. It's just conditioning right now," added Mary.

"Loves, continue on. What do you have scheduled afterwards?"

"Ah, come on, Mom. We have the Peace Model of Interrogation module up next, then a break. Help us," Mark pleaded teasingly.

"That's an important module. We'll meet after, to catch up. Go finish your PT, and don't make me look bad, or I'll compete with you myself. You don't want to be shown up by your aging momma." I winked.

"You and what army?!" Matthew added, laughing.

"Get. I brought you into this world, I can take you out. See you later," I stated with big grin, blowing a kiss as I turned around to make a call while walking towards the office.

Jake and Tom were already in the office. We got ahold of Steve to confirm there was no threat with his safety and instructed him to get on the road ASAP. Bethany shut the door. Tom came over to kiss me and pulled out a chair.

"Jake, you ok? You gave us quite the scare."

"Scared the shit out of me, too, and I'm trained for this."

"Poor judgment, or lack of judgment from alcohol?"

"A bit of both, if I'm being honest, but what are odds someone knew where/how/when we could be compromised?"

"Apparently, pretty high…"

We spent the next hour going over what had transpired, our mystery woman, and next action points. Steve finally showed up, looking worse for wear. Doug was a close friend to both the boys, and it was weighing heavy on them, as well. It was clear there were too many particulars to follow up on in a short time, and not enough manpower. Tom looked at me and asked, "Is it your intention to enlist your overseas friends?"

I nodded. "I called them just before I entered here. They're on board and making arrangements as we speak."

Bessum and Lily were cousins and had assisted me on my last mission. Bessum ("Bes") was the head of the Albanian mafia, while Lily was in charge of the Sicilian family, with her husband incarcerated for life. You didn't want to mess with them, especially Lily, who had some kinky sexual perverted thing going on with her victims—but they were like extended family, now. *Holy shit.*

"What about Freddy? Have you updated him?" Bethany probed.

"I'll fill him in when we leave. He's still on the mend, so we may use him as a command post to filter communications, and he'll need to assist in other areas. We have a Thucydides Trap, here, and America needs to bring on their A game. That's us."

Tom looked a little confused. "Forgive my ignorance, but what kind of trap?"

Bethany was quick to pipe in. "The simple version is when China and US are heading to war and China threatens to displace an existing power, the United States."

"So, worst possible outcome imaginable. Ok, got it."

"Oh, we're not going to just quote *Armageddon*. We're going to bring it. Let's get going. We leave at 0600. B, prep the plane. You'll be dropping Tom and me off first, then the boys. Jake, inform Ainsworth that, as of now, this facility is on high alert until otherwise noted. Steve, for the love of god, try to sober up."

With that, Tom and I eagerly went to go meet up with the kids.

FIVE

Texas

BETHANY DROPPED TOM AND I OFF at Northwest Regional Airport, near the Texas Motor Speedway in Ft. Worth. It was twenty minutes, max, from our ranch house. The kids weren't too happy about the limited time we spent with them, but understood the circumstances. Leaving them continues to be the hardest thing we ever do, even more so than tracking and killing punk-ass-no-good terrorists.

Freddy met us on the tarmac in his Chevy High Country Suburban with its three-inch lift and brush guard. He was taking Texas living to heart. Of course, it had some custom modifications, and after being shot at close range, it was understandable why he was a little skittish. I was surprised that he could hoist himself up into it, but that electric running board aided in boosting him up. I was just glad the guest house was one story, and I didn't have to put one of those chair lifts in it that you see on TV.

Having Freddy as my commander and surrogate father had been challenging, but nothing prepared us for the caretaking that ensued after his release from the hospital. I jokingly reminded him that (1) I never saw his face until two years ago, and that wasn't necessarily a bad thing, and (2) we were not equipped for "elderly care." We saw how his slow physical progress was affecting his mental clarity *and ability. Damn, no wonder why I'm all messed up after witnessing this.* I can attest that it's challenging to care for the elderly, and you recognize what a poor job American society is doing with this demographic.

"None of the team even came out to check on me. Hell, not even a wave hello?" he incredulously inquired as we threw our gear in the back cargo area. Upon reflection, we should have made time for them to visit. Freddy had been cooped up here, alone, for the most part, as we could not risk him getting infected by the virus in his current state of health.

"That's my bad, Freddy. No time for them to chit-chat; they were needed in other places. They send their best, if that makes you feel any better."

"Well, now, that gives me a warm and fuzzy. Shit, it's apparent that I don't pay the bills anymore."

"We can rectify that, if you like," I retorted with a Cheshire grin.

"Just kill me now," he said.

We unloaded, (in truth, Tom did most of it) and I grabbed a bottle of 2016 Château Pape Clément Pessac-Léognan to sit outside by the fire, with a nice charcuterie board, with Freddy. The two guest houses backed up to the main house, all sharing a common backyard/courtyard. Freddy had moved in while we brought in specialists to help him mend. Part of me has speculated that he just gave up. For decades, he was working to protect me and my secret identity, all the while being part of the root of 'our' entanglements and estrangements with others. Quite simply, he had checked out. With his wealth of knowledge and contacts, I needed him to check back in. Despite preferring to work alone, I understood that he was and always would be an extension of me. I needed him to get back on the horse, so to speak. Even if it meant me prodding him to do so.

"Do we know, yet, who the mystery woman was at the bar?" he started.

"We pulled up video surveillance from the hotel. No match in facial recognition. She was not registered there, and we see where she leaves Jake stumbling into the elevators as she turns to exit the building. From there, we tapped into the patrol cameras and caught her on I-70 to DIA. No trace of her at airport, but we do have complete photo recognition of her now, moving forward. Jake is following up on her."

"You were right there at DIA. Did you investigate?"

"We didn't have that intel at the time we departed."

"You know about the theories behind DIA, right?" Freddy continued.

Ever since the Denver International Airport was built 1995, there has been widespread speculation and theories. "Blucifer,' the blue demon horse with glowing red eyes, is considered to be a nod to the Four Horsemen. It was created at the entrance of the airport by a famed Mexican artist, only to have the sculpture fall on him before completion and cause his death. But, that's not what Freddy was alluding to.

He was talking about how the airport was built by the New World Order (with ties to Nazism), an organization we had more than a few run-ins with, over the years. The runways appear to be in design of a swastika, and is again theorized to be the Illuminati headquarters, with a secret underground lair in exchange for capital for the completion of the airport. The underground is equipped with tunnels and bunkers and is rumored to serve as a safe place in event of an apocalypse.

"You know who was affiliated with the Illuminati?"

"You talking about famous stars? Or that bitch Carter – may she rest in hell. Only fitting that our pal Fareed killed her. Remind me, didn't you hook up with her?"

"Lock it up, youngster. That was part of an ugly assignment."

Sure...

Carter, an unattractive sexual deviant in her own right, was the previous Deputy Director of the CIA. She was an identical twin to a stillborn sibling and partnered with others in an elaborate quest to use artificial technology to create a New World Order...exactly what this new virus was mimicking. Her death led us to the infiltration and compromise within several US agencies, including the CIA, DEA, NSA...shit, practically anything ending with an "a". We had inside help from unknowing CIA Directors Sedlin and Long, and FBI Director Coles. These guys were lifelong loyal patriots to America, not to a political party.

I came to trust them, but you had to question if they were still in these positions due to incredible ability to play the system, or if it was due to lack of ability, that they could be easily manipulated...just saying. I kept them close, but also at arm's length.

"What's your play?" he asked me as we watched the flames rise.

"Divide and conquer."

"Who is going where?"

"Bes is heading to Russia, Lily to China, Jake will follow-up with mystery lady, and Steve/Bethany/Tom will be on transportation, communication, and weapons procurement."

"You're sending Lily back to China? Remember what she did to Wang? I think she liked that. Yikes," he said with a cringe and a shiver.

"That's exactly why I'm sending her back. She won't fuck around. Wait, scratch that, you know what I mean." We both winced and laughed at the same time. I *almost* spit out my wine.

"Hmm. And us?" he continued.

"We need you back in the game. It's time. No more excuses, old man. You and I are heading to DC. You're going to meet up our pal at the FDA, and I'm meeting our favorite lobbyist and our pals at the FCC."

SIX

Russia

MANY COUNTRIES HAVE WANTED, contemplated, and even prayed for the demise of the United States. They feel that way about China now, also, for different reasons. At the heart of any back story, Russia has always been that foe to the United States. It's *Rocky IV* on steroids (and, let's be honest, most of them were probably on steroids when they made that movie.)

Can you name the last five Russian presidents? Well, probably not the best question to ask, as most Americans can't name the last five US presidents, either. Food for thought. Well, you'd have to have a good memory or understanding of Russian politics, as Vladimir Putin has been present since 1999 with the exception of a short reprieve of four years from 2008-2012 by Dmitry Medvedev. Dmitry now serves as Deputy of Security Council.

Know what Medvedev and Putin have in common with Napoleon? I believe the correct term is "vertically challenged."

All are short men and are well below the "published" average height of 5'10 men. (Napoleon was actually considered of "average height" for his time...sure, pal...)

Bes wasn't investigating Putin or Medvedev, but was looking into Gazprom, which owns gas processing facilities all over Russia. Oil. (Dammit, have to get that old *Beverly Hillbillies* intro song out of my head...*Oil, baby, black crude*...) Unlike capitalistic companies in the US, the Russian government holds fifty percent of Gazprom shares. You can see the conflict of interest, right?

Gazprom has over 100 subsidiaries, with the majority owned with one hundred percent investment. Refer back to who owns fifty percent. We were interested in Gazprom-Media, under the direction of Heinrich Snape, which is interesting, as he was German in origin. Heinrich translates to "rules an estate," and Snape translates to "outrage, dishonor, disgrace." Guess that's why he left Germany? Who knows?

Bes was set up to monitor Heinrich and his executive council to infiltrate how they disseminated media to influence and persuade the general public. After all, they had perfected this technique since 1947 and the start of the Cold War.

How can you discern a good Russian (insert any country) citizen versus a bad one when they have been manipulated by media? (i.e., during Vladimir Lenin's rule, who brainwashed the way of thinking of the communist party. Or the 'good' Germans, who did nothing to hurt Jews, but also nothing to help them?)

The same is happening in America, where the general population is directed and controlled by media/social media to accept irrational, unconstitutional, and unprecedented actions against their freedom(s). Permissions are now taken with social platforms that are censoring our fundamental freedom of speech and erasing/deleting anything that contradicts "their" perception of reality. Boiled down to simplicity, it impacts their bottom lines... Gates, Elon, Bezos, Zuckerberg, Buffet *(why are all referred to by their last names except Elon?)*.

Our forefathers could not predict, could not fathom, that the richest people in America would have hundreds of BILLIONS of dollars. In fact, it's not addressed in the 27 Amendments. Over two hundred years, and no legislation has been added to really address and tackle this. Our government intervened in the 1980s, with the breakup of ATT over monopolistic power, with an antitrust lawsuit. Little refresher here, for you: antitrust law is both the federal and state government laws that regulate big business to promote competition…wait for it…for the benefit of consumers. Yeah, that ship has passed. Interestingly enough, the longest addressed amendment which was ratified in 1992 is Amendment 27 – Congressional Compensation.

"WTF are you doing calling at this hour?" Bes answered with a few more choice words in a language I wasn't fluent in.

"My bad. Forgot about that nine-hour time difference, but since you're up now, any new intel to share?"

"I've killed for less reason than this."

"Me too. And your point?"

Silence.

He laughed. *Whew.*

"It hasn't even been twenty-four hours. I'm not Jesus."

"That, my friend, is correct. He had hair."

"Wake me up before dawn AND give me shit. I know where your children are…"

"I yield."

Every person has a breaking point. He just hit mine. Point to Bessum. *Mental note to make sure I was tracking his kids…just in case.*

"Since I'm up now anyways, I'll call after I brew a pot."

We went over the surveillance he'd put in place, the extraction methods of intel, and the team he had following the executive members. Feeling confident of the timeline, I reminded him that this was an exploratory mission, and direct interference or confrontation should be avoided at all costs (or at least kept to a minimum).

"I'll attempt to accommodate, but let's agree to disagree. I'll handle things how I see fit," he flatly stated.

It wasn't really up for negotiation.

SEVEN

China

SINCE I HAD ALREADY AWOKEN BES, I figured that now would be a good time to check in with Lily, also. Lily had a bigger task, of the two of them, and would be infiltrating (1) the National Medical Products Administration (NMPA), which is the Chinese equivalent to our FDA and (2) Chinese media.

In 2008, the FDA created a Chinese office in Beijing to serve as a principal office to regulate the products produced in China for export to the US. Despite having an office on location, the US is in the dark on what Chinese facilities are producing. One of the biggest concerns is the lack of information on distribution levels and production levels of API (Active Pharmaceutical Ingredient) for any drug, as US pharmaceutical companies rely on production overseas.

In addition to not being able to monitor outsourced production, which accounts for roughly 70% of our supply, it demonstrates how vulnerable the US is in the pharmaceutical market due to dependency on foreign countries. China is known to cut corners, and is not concerned with consumer protection laws or product liability. It has constant recall on products that have been distributed for years.

Remember the equation 1.4 billion people versus 328 million? We simply don't have the resources to check every product prior to entry, and must weigh results versus the effects. You witness this daily. You see ads for "X" (let's use bipolar medicine as an example), and they spend the entire time listing the potential side effects as a limited warranty from potential lawsuits. It's ALWAYS about the bottom line.

The World Health Organization (WHO) started reporting virus cases and deaths months after the confirmation of the release of the virus. The WHO is run by China and financed heavily by US (until now), so there's some conflict of interest going on, here. Much speculation and debate in terms of length of timing and accurate reporting was questioned of the organization, by the world. With every nation looking for accurate reporting of China's fatalities, China simply elected to stop reporting. Statistically their numbers were not computing. China's total deaths per million were reported at sixty-one verses two hundred fifty-seven worldwide average. Or, let's make it easier to visualize. The US had more than 788,000 deaths to date compared to China's reporting of only 4,600. See why there are concerns about China manufacturing a weapon against the US? *If you don't...seek help...immediately...for the love of God.*

But, there was more at play here. There always is. If this wasn't a Chinese insurgency gone wrong, then who and what else was targeted? Enter Three Gorges Dam on the Yangtze River in China, which started construction in1994 and concluded in 2006. It is the largest and most productive dam in the world. Based on the building specs, environmentalists feared the dam would trigger earthquakes and landslides due to large amounts of water in the reservoir, and if there were any collapse in structure, it would impact 1.9 million people and over 1,500 cities.

As the world dealt with a deadly virus, hurricanes, and murder hornets, China was also experiencing record floods themselves and was nearing capacity, opening conjecture about a potential collapse.

It would be embarrassing for China at epic levels, and was something they would avoid at all costs. Remember the coverup of Chernobyl? Get ready for part deux, times ten. With satellite imaging and new technology, China would not be able to conceal if it broke, but they could and would control the media coverage, which they own hands down.

Instead of a manufacturing error, how about a terrorist attack? Act of God? Ooh, how about Rods of God? A kinetic energy metal made from Tungsten, about the size of a telephone pole projectiled from space? Insert whatever the fuck they want, here. Or, if we are being nefarious and more realistic, what if they or a third-party pins it on the US? Kaboom.

Most of the US media outlets have strong financial ties to China, with the Chinese Communist Party (CCP) impersonating the government's propaganda and coverups. Why do US companies allow this? *Financial reasons.* Again, it's ALWAYS about money.

There are five levels of threat, the lowest being green and the highest being red. The top five threats consist of: terrorism, espionage, proliferation, economic espionage, and targeting the national information infrastructure. Technically, we are already in WWIII as we fight biological and cyber warfare crimes against America. The US population continues to play willful ignorance.

"Yes," is how Lily answered the call; not… "Good morning, how you doing? This is Lily, how may I help you…" *I hope I never encounter her in a dark alley.*

"Just checking in. I assume there's nothing to report, but wanted to go over any logistics we need to supply on our end."

"You assumed wrong. I have a meeting with Li Qiang this afternoon."

Li was the NMPA Commissioner and number two on leadership team. Li = pretty, powerful. Qiang = strong or can mean gun. So, f'ing strong or powerful gun was what his name meant. Just great.

"Good news. Lily…we are gathering information only. Umm, this goes without saying, but let's try to avoid any Wang repeats…" Wang was the last guy she'd strangulated during "roleplay," mutilating him to the point that even dental records couldn't be used to identify him.

"You have your ways of getting information, I have mine."

Good chat.

No use arguing this point. And that's why I have always stated I was more fearful of women than men, in life. Men might physically be able to dominate (not generally the case with me), but a woman would patiently wait while they psychologically messed you up to a point of no return.

You've heard those stories where the fiancé finds out her soon-to-be husband had an affair, and she waits until the wedding day to tape pictures of him under the guest's chairs having sex with the stranger so everyone can witness? And that's the average woman.

Lily was the head of the Sicilian mafia, with her husband incarcerated. She's not your average woman, and she was pissed as this virus was shutting down her economy.

EIGHT

Washington, D.C.

BETHANY DROPPED JAKE OFF in DC once facial recognition picked up our mystery woman leaving Dulles airport. From there, he scoured hours of video footage to track her before she popped up again, sans disguise...at the Capitol, of all places.

"Hey, Matti, you ready for this?"

"Shoot, let's hear it."

"Bethany is on the way back to get you and Freddy, ETA three hours. Looks like we are looking for the same person."

"You lost me. I'm not following."

"Our mystery lady is Chanlor Wilson. The same lobbyist you're wanting to meet, right?"

"That would be one in the same."

"Well, get ready, then."

"Shit. I assume you mean Bethany returning, more so than dealing with Chanlor?"

"She's hot about having to make two back-to-back trips."

"This day just keeps getting better...."

Bethany returned to take Freddy and I back to DC. For three hours, we had to listen to her complain. There wasn't enough alcohol on the plane. Just saying.

Once all our gear was loaded in Jake's SUV, Bethany wasted no time getting wheels up. She waved to us, I think with one finger, as we entered our car. Despite all her balking, I think she enjoyed having the extra alone flying time.

We dropped Freddy off at The Capitol Hill Hotel, which had a mid-century modern vibe, calligraphy art, and a quiet location. The hotel is also within walking distance of the Supreme Court, Library of Congress, and National Mall. It was a thirty-minute commute from the FDA White Oak campus, but Freddy would be taking meetings on the Hill. Jake and I would be at the St Regis, just on the opposite side of the Capitol. I wanted the team to separate after the failed attempt in Vail.

Jake and I were sitting in the bar at Charlie Palmer Steak House, a popular lobbyist hangout with an impressive wine display as a centerpiece—a raw bar of oysters, crab, shrimp, lobster, and Wagyu steak that will hurt your pocketbook. The cheese cart was divine. Luckily, most people who frequented here were on an expense budget (and that's why the American government pays $5000 for a toilet, folks).

I had just ordered their Dirty Politics martini, but with Ketel One vodka and their house-made pickle juice, and substituted jalapeno olives for the blue cheese. Jake was opting for a mocktail, needing to keep his wits around this broad.

"Think she'll show tonight?" he asked earnestly.

"Getting butterflies?"

"More like rage. She tried to kill me."

"Patience. By the way, she tried to kill all of us," I said flatly.

"Before I punch her thick skull in, I just want to know why."

"That won't be necessary. She had no other option."

"How do you know?" he asked pensively.

"Women's intuition. Someone has something on her. Desperate people do desperate things. You liked her, didn't you? Is that why you are so agitated?"

"She tried to kill me. I got over it, but yes, the prospects of having someone and not being the only one by myself in this shitshow of a group did have a certain appeal."

"Oh, Jake. You're not alone. Remember that. You always have your left hand," I teased, trying to lighten the mood.

"God dammit, Matti, I don't know why I bother."

"Ooh, look to your right. 3:00. Bingo. Wait... *there's one perfect fit, And, sugar, this one is it; we both are so excited 'cause we're reunited, hey, hey... "*

"You can just die. Fuck you and Peaches and Herb," he retorted, disgusted, shaking his head.

Chanlor was a very attractive woman, same height as me, with deep brown eyes, long luscious brown hair, and incredible eyebrows that would be hard to transform in disguise. She was wearing a cream-colored Tom Ford, strong shoulder, double-breasted pant suit, with a black camisole underneath, with black Christian Louboutin suede pumps. Practical, refined, but also made the statement, "I'm one to be reckoned with." I was starting to like this chick.

"It's go time. Meet you at the car," I said as I laid down cash for our bill, to exit.

Jake circled the room as he waited to approach from behind at the right moment. I waited and watched by the front door to ensure no surprises, my Sig Sauer Legion RXP compact in proximity. *Just give me a reason.*

Jake grabbed her left elbow and turned her slowly towards him. Her eyes widened in shock and fear as she recognized him and, more importantly, comprehended that he recognized her. Her hand was shaking as she held her drink.

"Please, take a last sip. There's probably nothing in it. No guarantees, though."

Her face contorted now, fear mixing with hesitation while she calculated her next steps. She was a damn lobbyist, after all, the kings (and queens) of impromptu debate.

"This is a very public place," she whispered as she decided against taking a sip.

"You tried to kill me; do you really think I care?"

"Let me grab my coat."

"Nice try. You didn't enter with one." He took her drink from her hand, downed it, and put it on the table more forcefully now, with his hand on the small of her back, directing her to the door.

"Please...let me explain," she urged with more hushed, anxious whispers.

"Look up and smile; we're on camera," he said as they proceeded out the door.

NINE

JAKE DIRECTED CHANLOR to the driver's side of the SUV. She was visibly confused when he told her to get in and drive, then became fearful when she saw my figure in the back seat, with my Sig pointed at her head. Perspiration trickled down her Tom Ford suit.

Jake took his time walking around the car to enter the passenger's side door. She fearfully looked at me in the rearview mirror, hands at ten and two on the steering wheel. She said nothing.

"Drive," Jake commanded.

"Where to?" she asked, her voice was quivering, hands trembling.

"To whomever gave you the order."

"Please. Please. They will kill me. They've threatened my mother in her nursing home."

She was telling the truth. A quick search showed that Chanlor had contacted the police three months ago to report her penthouse apartment broken into and her cat skinned alive and left pinned to the wall above her bed. That's messed up. The police dismissed it and said she wasn't targeted, as there were four other similar events that same night. The other victims were random, across town. No connection, per the police.

There's always a connection. The desperately random events just shows that they tried too hard to make it look random. Even Starling knew this in *Silence of the Lambs*.

"Drive to the Capital Hilton by long way of the monuments," Jake instructed. The Hilton was less than two miles from Charlie's and across the street from St. Regis, but Jake was having her drive the long way as we waited and observed if anyone following. Chanlor was digressing quickly with each passing moment.

"Any time now, Ms. Wilson. For your own preservation, I suggest you start from the beginning," I said flatly.

Tears were streaming down her face, her head shaking back and forth as she contemplated how she got here in the first place, calculating her next thoughts with white knuckles clutching the wheel.

Finally, she started. "It was just another day. My firm was asked to assist in fast tracking new regulations on approval processes and timelines for new vaccines. It starts with generating public comments, which are submitted to a public docket. We assisted in flooding it with "generated responses."

"So, you provided fake intel and…"

"Once the FDA receives public comments and decides what further action is needed, they issue a final rule which explains requirements and impact, but before it can become final-final, it may be reviewed by other parts of the federal government.

"That's where the unexpected 'hiccup' originated. A non-health and human services agency was assigned to consult before it could be published. Roman Wagner, the FDA Commissioner, went ballistic, and it's gone downhill since then.

"I have known Wagner for years as a long-standing family friend. I mean, our families are the best of friends. Yacht, trips, you name it. I simply didn't realize what he was originally asking, or the implications. I thought I was just doing a favor. I didn't comprehend or envision that he would use me." She had a finality in her voice as she laid out the events.

"Let's start off with a few questions, and that will dictate how we proceed. First, why did they target us?" I noticed Jake was looking at her skeptically, but also with a tinge of longing. I was secretly praying that I didn't have to blow her brains out in front of him.

"Wagner got wind that your team was ordered by the President to investigate, and knew that would result in a halt. Your reputation proceeds you, and a woman declared dead would not have any qualms."

Zero Dark Thirty all over. Once you're on a list, you're never off of it.

"Who gave you the intel that we were in Vail?"

"He did. Well, I guess it was him. All I know is that I was given information three days prior to your arrival, and steps to take to make it look like an accident. They gave me a point person with a valet. They told me I just had to slip something in the drinks of the drivers, and the contact told me who the recipients were. I had no idea what it was or what it did. They showed me pictures of my mom's nursing home, with someone holding a knife up to her throat while she was sleeping. My mother! Someone whom he had vacationed with, and came to visit in the home after my father left. He said this was the final thing I needed to assist with, or they'd kill more than just my cat. I had no choice. It was my mom!"

Three days before…are you f'in kidding me?!

"Ms. Wilson…"

Before I could finish the sentence, she had already interrupted. "Please don't kill me. There's no one else to take care of my mother," she pleaded, begging on the brink of hysteria with real tears running down her face. Jake sat motionless, watching.

"Calm yourself. When were you contacted, or when was your firm initially hired for this project?"

A state of confusion emerged as she tried to process the impact of her answer, or its significance. She looked at Jake, who was stone-faced, and then back to me in the rearview.

"This nightmare started two years ago."

That's what I was afraid of. More than one year before the virus hit. Explains why the President wanted me to investigate.

Houston, we have a problem.

TEN

THE WORLD AS WE KNOW IT had succumbed to 'confirmation bias', being the tendency to favor and interpret new evidence that confirms your own existing (often unfounded) beliefs. In fact, you tend to ignore any contrary information. Add in artificial intelligence with its sophisticated algorithms, and it now reinforces your preconceived beliefs with more like-minded intelligence...

You're in a whole world of hurt, making it almost damn near impossible to change your mind or direction. The irony is...most people *think* they're not like other people.

You've witnessed this with police, doctors, and your oil change. You seek help from a trusted and/or respected individual/organization and tell them of your dilemma (you saw a masked man whom you think was black steal from your car; your ACL is torn; you think you have an oil leak).

In the first scenario, you've already framed the evidence by pointing out that the person was hiding their face and was possibly of color. (You have no data to confirm the perp's color, and an obvious reason is that the criminal didn't want to be recognized, but who cares about facts? Let's go with biased emotion...)

Reinforced with statistical averages for that particular neighborhood, the police are now searching for a POC to fit that description versus treating all data equally. This can also fall in the category of statistical bias, which results in you over- or under-estimating a parameter based on statistical information. (i.e - Black people in X neighborhood account for 40% of the crime, but have 14% of the population; therefore, the probability of X crime is statistically higher for POC in this area.)

What the hell am I talking about?

Well, let's talk about our friends over at the Transportation Security Administration (TSA). After 9/11, TSA was the central agency for the security of the FAA, airlines, and airports. Last year, their budget was over eight billion dollars. If you are a male or person of any color, traveling alone, with no checked bags but a backpack, I'll give you 1000-to-1 odds that you will be searched. Why? Is it inherent "systematic" prejudice or profiling? Not all Muslims are terrorists, but 92% of worldwide terrorism is caused by Muslims. Not so fast…you must take into consideration your sampling pool to avoid errors, as 95% of the terrorist-related deaths occurred in the Middle East, Africa, and South Asia.

US public opinion is so extreme over concerns of threat of terrorism that we fail to acknowledge simple truths (that terrorism accounts for less than .05% of global deaths, and despite what you are led to believe, airline high jackings are very rare, today).

So, why all the fear? 24/7 media coverage, which is disproportionate to the actual circumstances. Confirmation bias.

Enter the Federal Communications Commission (FCC). The FCC is an independent federal agency charged with implementing and enforcing US communications laws and regulations…and technological innovation. One of their key initiatives is to revise media regulations so that new technologies flourish alongside diversity and localism. Their largest initiative is high-speed internet and wireless connectively to 5G (which I have stated for the record, for years now, that is already an outdated technology).

The agency leadership of five commissioners is appointed by the President of the US and confirmed by the Senate. Under them, they have bureaus for Consumer & Governmental Affairs, Enforcement, International, Media, Public Safety/Homeland, Wireless Telecommunications, and Wireline Competition.

I needed intel from Public Safety/Homeland Security bureau chief Kelly Davidson. Damn, another woman to contend with. Davidson had the smallest staff under her, of all the bureau chiefs, and in my humble opinion, held the greatest threat risk to our nation under her authority. Cybersecurity.

Most Americans are unaware of Project Mockingbird under President JFK. This was authorized wiretapping by CIA to understand how the press obtained classified information, and to determine how they obtained and leaked it to the public. Involved were the Director of the CIA, the US Attorney General, the Secretary of Defense, and the Director if Intelligence Agency.

So, pretty much everyone; and they were found blameless in their attempts because they engaged and violated warrantless surveillance to determine the source of the leak. Had they reported that their objective was to obtain foreign intelligence, they would have been fine. Bureaucracy at its best. I've often stated that politicians should be limited to two terms.

You assume I was referring to years, but actually, one term in office, and one term in prison. Just saying.

ELEVEN

THE GOVERNMENT OF THE UNITED STATES

YOU KNOW WHAT I SEE when I look at this organizational chart? The reason why taxes are so high.

Know what agency you do not see? The US Food and Drug Administration (FDA). It falls under the Department of Health and Human Services. The FDA not only regulates food, but human and veterinary drugs, medical devices, biological products...and vaccines.

Roman Wagner was the dinosaur that had been the FDA Commissioner and worked his way up the ranks over the decades. He felt that he was a loyal patriot, and should be in his position based on his long-standing merits. He was old-school in his mentality, but was obviously learning and picking up a few despicable tricks, with his latest methods. He only respects woman, in that they have a place in the home. His poor wife. (Well, third wife. The other two managed to bank a few dollars before they left.)

Freddy and Roman were about the same age, and had previous working relations on covert operations. What? FDA has covert operations? Yes, don't be so damn naïve. Any intelligence operation that is designed to conceal the identity of the party (agency) and is used to create a political result with repercussions in military, intelligence, or law affecting the population of a country or individuals/countries outside of it, is considered 'covert'.

Per their own guidelines, *"The FDA's mission to protect and promote the public health requires that the FDA remain prepared to deal with a wide variety of natural and manmade threats that involve, impact, or require the use of FDA-regulated products."*

We were dealing with a manmade threat with unconfirmed accusations of the generating or participating entity or country.

The FDA has roughly 15,000 employees, with an annual budget over three billion. To give a reference on the sheer size of a disquieting problem, there are 9.1 million federal government 'workers': 2.1 million full-time federal employees, 4.1 million contract, 1.2 million grant, 1.3 million active military, and half a million postal employees.

The US government just handed out over four trillion in bailout resources (more than we spent in twenty years on the Afghanistan war—and, incidentally, we lost almost the exact same number in that war as we did in 9-11 attack).

It's unfortunate that the American public was not the largest benefactor of this bailout, receiving less than twenty percent of the total. The public was not informed that the JFK Performing Arts Center received twenty-five million in the latest bail out relief fund (or sixty percent of their annual budget, for the maintenance of an establishment no one could enter due to the virus…well, except the federal employees who work there and were on mandatory leave…). There was also five billion allotted for Opioid treatment…that other silent pandemic in the US.

Anyways.

Freddy was at Filomena's restaurant, which was located minutes from his hotel. This was Bethany's and my favorite place, with a little old grandma at the front entrance hand rolling divine pasta, so I prayed he wouldn't do anything to screw up our favorite restaurant. We had CIA Directors Sedlin and Long there, to observe and record. Picture Sedlin and Long as Sgt. Taggart and Detective Rosewood from *Beverly Hills Cop*. Nice guys, but…Just saying. In the current cancel culture environment with fact suppression and censorship by big media, we needed much visual and recorded confirmation, if we were to be successful in changing the narrative.

I gave Freddy my Glock 34 Gen 5 with Combat Master package that I'd had my friends at Taran Tactical custom make for me. I hated lending out my personal gear, as it had a way of never returning. Tom, Steve, and Bethany were busy supplying Bes and Lily with other custom weaponry, so I took from my private stash for Freddy and myself. I don't know the last time Freddy actually had to use a weapon. The problem with "management." Told him that, if in doubt, he was shoot first and often and ask later; but no matter what, make sure Grandma (who makes our favorite pasta) doesn't get hit.

Freddy was inside sitting down, waiting for Wagner to arrive with me in his earpiece. "He's still not here, I'll wait another hour, at max," he stated.

"Please tell me you're being somewhat discreet talking, so people don't think you are insane or see you. I know it's been a hot minute since you have done this."

"I've been doing this longer than you have years on this earth. Lock it up."

"Order some damn wine to pass the time."

"What do you recommend?"

"Order the Luce della Vite, it's delicious."

"I don't see it on menu. Wait, it's only offered by the bottle, and is $450. Are you kidding?"

"Umm, no. One: you're not paying for it; and two, you can cork it and bring with you when you bring out Wagner."

"Jesus Christ."

"Hey, now: you're in an Italian restaurant, which is second to church."

"Keep it up, I'll turn this earpiece off."

"Bitch, bitch, bitch."

Freddy sipped slowly as he waited and waited. I debated about ordering some Agnolotti alla Carbonara to bring out to the car, but reluctantly opted out. Sedlin and Long took liberties to order several courses while they waited it out—on my tab, of course.

Finally, at 9:30 pm, Wagner and wifey number three strolled in and sat down four tables away from Freddy.

"It's go time…here comes your resurrection, Freddy, make it good. No pressure. Make sure to grab that wine, too."

"Take notes," was all he responded as I heard him pay the bill and grab his jacket.

Roman looked like a Roman to me, if that makes sense. But, he had short blonde hair and was 5'8—not heavy, but what you might call stout. Maybe he looked more Czechoslovakian. Regardless, wifey number three was 32 years old. She didn't marry him for his looks or sweet demeanor. We were counting on this.

I only had audio, so relied on Sedlin to inform me if my presence was needed as a last resort. I heard Freddy walking to the table. "Hello Roman, good to see you again."

No immediate reply. Freddy, after all, was declared dead. Roman had even attended Freddy's very public funeral. I'm confident that he was lost, trying to calculate and process.

"My word, Freddy. I'm speechless," was all he could muster.

"Good evening. I'm Fred Johnson, and old work friend of your husband's. My apologies for interrupting your dinner, but we have some high-security items that need his immediate attention."

"Oh, wow! I never get to meet Roman's work friends, so this is a treat. Does he need to leave now?"

Before Roman could respond, Freddy was quick to add, "I wish we didn't have to, but I'm going to need to steal him for a bit. Please try the Agnolotti alla Carbonara. And I just opened this bottle that you must try. There're two gentlemen over in that far corner that will be glad to assist you home when you are done."

"Fred, um…can't this wait 'til after dinner?"

At that point, I'm sure Fred showed or indicated the bulge in his pocket *(the gun, you twisted sicko)* and simply said it was a matter of national emergency. Roman was out of options, telling his wife he'd see her at home while Freddy assisted in gathering his things.

How apropos: the Eagle's *Lying Eyes* came on just as Roman was gathering his things… *You can't hide your lyin' eyes, and your smile is a thin disguise. I thought by now you'd realize, there ain't no way to hide your lyin' eyes…*

I could faintly hear wifey in the background, happily pouring my wine into her glass.

TWELVE

"IF I KNEW YOU'D GIVE AWAY THE WINE, I would have selected a more appropriate bottle," I whispered to Freddy as he escorted Wagner out to the car.

"My bad," his short response.

Sounded like Freddy was getting some of his mojo back. Good for him; about damn time.

"Well, well, aren't we full of surprises?" Roman said when he saw me as he entered the back seat of the SUV.

"Good evening, Mr. Wagner. If you'll oblige us," I said as I handed over a black face mask to cover his head.

"Are you kidding me?" he inquired earnestly.

"You can do it, or I can do it for you," I answered as I continued to move the mask closer within his reach.

"You will live to regret this," he threatened as he grabbed it reluctantly and placed it over his head.

"I already do." And with that, I knocked him the f'out.

The concoction I administered Wagner would ensure a deep slumber for at least 18 hours. Bethany had the plane prepped and ready to take Freddy, Jake, and our comatose guest back to Texas. Jake also brought Wilson on board, stating it was for her protection.

I think he was wanting to use some other type of "protection." It was better to have all the parties with us, so I had no arguments.

I was staying on to sort out some unfinished business. Once Freddy and I resurfaced, it was only a matter of time. We would be like *Bourne Identity,* and everyone would be targeting us to put in a body bag to shield any association or connection from past (or future) operations.

I had intel from Davidson that I still needed to follow up on, and she reluctantly agreed to meet me at the St Regis Bar. When a dead person calls you to meet up, you should probably meet them. She concurred.

The hotel is grandiose and ornate in every sense, giving way to a period piece from the early 1900s outside, with red awnings. Gold trim mirrored the inside red velvet couches, and gold finished ceilings rivaled The Vatican. It truly resonated with a blessed life.

Due to the virus and extreme travel restrictions, I was able to secure the Presidential Suite with butler service. I had called ahead and had my Chiara Boni, satin lapel, long-sleeve jumpsuit steamed. The only downside to my attire is that it limited my ability to conceal any weapons of choice on my body. I did have a saddle brown Valentino calfskin tote that had ample room for my Glock, that I took back from Freddy. My knee buckled two times while I was getting ready. It was a reminder of how badly I needed to go see the good Doc, sooner than later.

The St. Regis bar's signature drink is a take on the classic Bloody Mary, but I opted for a Deep Eddy's Lemon Cosmo with no twist for the evening as I sat waiting for Davidson's arrival.

Five minutes late and counting…I detested people who could not arrive on time. Tom gave me grief on this specific topic constantly, saying that not all people are wired in a militaristic, warped sense on time; to which I countered that they should be, otherwise they are demonstrating their lack of ability (or lack of respect).

Now I ask you: if someone can be elevated to be the position of Chair, Commissioner, or President, etc. and cannot arrive on time, then doesn't it simply mean they feel their time is more valuable than yours? Exactly. Just being rhetorical.

Davison strolled in ten minutes late. Bitch. She had long black hair pulled up in a sleek, high pony, allowing her to look slightly younger than her actual age. She did not have an extra ounce of fat to spare, and her file noted that she was a workout fanatic. That's the politically correct term the general public uses, versus…freak, obsessive, extreme. People who work out excessively usually fall into two categories: those that do so because that's the only area that they can control, or they have control issues in all areas of their lives. I was putting Davidson in the latter category.

"My apologies for being late. My Uber was stuck in traffic."

Why do people come up with lame excuses, thinking the other party will find them acceptable? She didn't respect my time, and had just confirmed she considered me an idiot, too. Big mistake; huge.

I grabbed her hands and turned them over, inspecting her fingers. She had a curious look on her face as I did this. Almost sexual. "Just wanted to make sure all your digits still worked," I said as I dropped her hands dismissively and motioned for her to take a seat. My point was made.

"My apologies. I'm nervous, and frankly, I don't know what to expect or do. That's why I was late, as I was stalling to try to figure this out.

"You have me in a precarious position. After you contacted me, I read up on the reports on your demise and of your infamous exploits, yet here you are in front of me, living and breathing. I'm not sure what to make of all of it, and the implications. I had known Freddy for a long time, as well. I attended his funeral."

"You should consider this a..." *I paused for effect...* "professional courtesy – woman-a-woman. But, please don't make the mistake of thinking it extends further than that. You have information that I need, and it would be prudent for you to understand the ramifications if it is not supplied, or is mistakenly provided incorrectly. A dead woman has no remorse."

"As if I have other viable options," she didn't hesitate to respond.

"How astute. Please order a drink, we're going to be here for a while."

She ordered a scotch, neat, while I interrogated her on the FCC and Homeland Security proceedings with cybersecurity and other associated parties. She verified that Russia and China had stakes, and had infiltrated all our platforms. She also verified it was with US consent, in some circumstances. She provided additional intel on USCybercom, which is a military branch that was created under NSA. We discussed at length the theft of hardware, software, and electronic data, and how it related to the manipulation of information in regard to the spread and treatment of the virus. It is fascinating how alarmingly ignorant the American public really is.

We were on drink number two, and I found her to be credible, perceptive, and even receptive to understanding the corollaries and tentacles of the national and worldwide impact of such collusion. Yet, she was the bureau chief, and had done nothing. This did not bode well for her.

We continued with the Q&A for another hour, and while coming to an end of our discussions and finishing drink number 3, I asked, "Who was most influential in getting you to this position?"

"That would be Nancy."

I sat stoned faced, as if I knew every Tom, Dick, and Harry in this city and understood who she was referring to, but played naïve.

"Sorry, drink 3. That came off as elitist. That would be Madam Secretary; or more accurately, now, acting President Adams."

"When was the last time you saw her?"

"Hmm. It was before the virus hit, so…actually…I believe it was at Freddy's funeral. I was in attendance with her, the FDA Commissioner, and a Chinese nationalist."

Wagner + Adams + Chinese = Time Bomb.

Did she just misstep in telling me this?

I paid the bill and told her I would be in touch. She grabbed my hands this time, and held onto them, looking at me longingly, a little too long. *Oh, shit.* With that last nugget, she asked what would happen next, and how should she proceed going forward? I told her to just do her job, and I'd be in touch. Her eyes lit up on the word "touch." I wondered if she had Peter Gabriel's *In Your Eyes* going through her head… *In your eyes, the light, the heat (in your eyes), I am complete (in your eyes); I see the doorway (in your eyes) …*

She'd only be seeing my backside as I fast-tracked it out the doorway and hauled it back to my room.

THIRTEEN

China

I HAD TOM GO THROUGH VIDEO FOOTAGE from both Freddy's and my funerals to see who was in attendance and, more importantly, to identify our Chinese Nationalist. Turns out, it was Li Bao, the son of Li Qiang. It always confuses foreigners that the first name in China is a Chinese person's last name. So, we had junior in attendance (or "powerful gun." as his name translates to). He looked like a little hit man, like Joe Pesci in *Goodfellas*. Key word: little.

Nepotism is fluent throughout all countries and the US has had its fair share of disgraced first children in positions of power based on "Daddy." I personally don't have an issue with this practice (after all, my own children are following suit), but…I'm not using my position to have my children involved in corrupt activities for monetized personal gains. I can't say that for others.

Sure, we've seen our fair share of Presidential children caught smoking pot, doing underage drinking, or ditching the Secret Service. Hell, Teddy Roosevelt's children brought a pony inside the White House to ride in the elevator. A little rebellion is to be expected of first children. Not my children. I'd kick their asses.

The Chinese have a different perspective on nepotism. Shocker. With the arrival of the virus and deaths of the US President and Vice

President, alarming messages came blaring over social media to spread the word that the US was attacking China, advising listeners to take measures to secure your homes in case of home invasions. Many of the sources cited the Department of Homeland Security (aka Davidson) in alarming the public that troops were in place. The erroneous messages were so widespread and damming that the White House Security Council issued an announcement over Twitter that they were fake. Twitter was now our official news vehicle. *Good lord.*

Reminded me of the movie *Murder at 1600* with Wesley Snipes, where the President is presented false evidence to illicit his resignation. Only, now, the US public was being offered false evidence to shut down the economy and sway future elections.

I had Tom cross-reference Bao's location and whereabouts and low and behold, he was in Vail at the same time of the Mexican nationalist's arrival. What are the odds, and why didn't we confirm that during our visit?

It was time to touch base with Lily. I hadn't received a status update from her. Not surprising. I reached her on an encrypted line, but we still kept texts to a minimum.

Me: Status update.

Lily: Going.

Me: More.

Lily: Alive.

Me: Li?

Lily: Alive.

Me: New intel?

Lily: Bigger cover-up.

Me: Specifics?

Lily: Planned obsolescence.

Me: Humans or technology?

Lily: Countries.

Me: US primary target?

Lily: Man in High Castle scenario.

Me: Options?

Lily: Start cutting heads off Medusa.

Me: Don't strike without confirmation.

Lily: "Offline."

In one respect, I admired Lily's attitude. On the other hand, we should all be afraid. Then again, she was right on this matter.

The virus provided another backstory and opportunity for the Chinese government. For years, they have been collecting DNA samples under Ancestry.com and 23andme-type applications. The Chinese already have your financial make-up; now they were using unique DNA profiles to create a multitude of scenarios. By analyzing DNA sequencing, they could predict medical outcomes and even thwart some…for a price.

I was tasked by the President to determine and stop the outcome(s). I was able to categorize my mission very easy. To save American lives at all costs.

There was no debate that the Chinese manufactured this virus. The debate comes to why. Which parties are nefarious, here? In my humble opinion…all of them. Greed will get you every time.

On paper, it appeared the Chinese used this as an opportunity to further reach their goals of world dominance by 2025. They now had the perfect combination of financial, economic, and personal information on billions of humans to accurately predict reactions and, more importantly, consequences.

How many times do you have to hear "THEY ARE IN IT TO WIN IT" and not understand the implications? Who is being obtuse?

Between riots, protests, BLM, and LGBTQIA (I must look up the correct acronym of that one each time), the United States had perfect diversions from the real issue – our dependence on China.

Acting President Adams had her own agenda, as do most of your elected officials. She wanted a legacy after she was gone. It had to be more than just the first acting US female President. The first predictions by Center for Disease Control had estimated US fatalities to be closer to 2 million. If that becomes true, let's play out a hypothetical scenario:

To date, there have been over 48 million US cases which China has access to (or can obtain information on), down to the smallest DNA fragment of each person.

Of the deaths caused by virus, over 95% are individuals 65 and older.

If we continue with this projection, China will have data on over 125 million, or roughly 1/3 of the US population.

How can the US afford the trillion-dollar handouts? Well, if we continue at this rate, there will be over 1.9 million elderly Americans who will no longer be with us. Nor will they receive the average $2800 in monthly social security benefits, going forward, and Medicare will become the next Blockbuster. Within just one year, from social security reductions alone, the US will save $63,840,000,000.

Robbing Peter to pay Paul. Never a good strategy.

This is just a simplified version of what could be. Once we determined the real version, it would be much scarier.

Lily may be bat shit crazy in her methods, but to fight our enemies, we needed to jump up to her level.

FOURTEEN

DC

AFTER REACHING OUT TO LILY, I decided a quick run would help clear my head and kick out the cobwebs. I also wanted to see if my left knee would hold up. I switched out my jumpsuit into some LuLu leggings with pockets, a hoodie, and my Hoka shoes, which I found to be the best for my left "Greek foot."

Morton's toe, otherwise known as "Greek foot," is when a person's second toe is larger than the first and fable, has it, is indicative of being a natural leader, having greater intelligence, and even a royal demeanor. Mine was the result of multiple surgeries, but no one really needed to know that.

I popped in one airbud, switched on the SiriusXm Classic Vinyl channel, and let the cool night wake me up. I headed south past Lafayette Square towards The Ellipse, a 52-acre park south of the White House which is named after the five-furlong circumference street within the park. Normally open to the public, it had been closed off due to the virus's restrictions.

It was ten at night. Not the best time to take a run in DC on any normal given day. The times were not normal, and DC has one of the highest crime rates in America, compared to all cities, regardless of size. The chance of being a victim of crime was recorded at one in seventeen.

The air was crisp, even invigorating, and I had a nice pace going. No world record pace, mind you, but faster than your average runner. It was 1.6 miles to get to The Ellipse via Constitution Ave, and (knock on wood) my knee was holding up with no issues. Of course, I wasn't doing squats, lunges, turning sharply, or anything else that could exacerbate this.

My mind was racing, trying to tie in what had transpired: the conversations, locations, missing dots, and long-term ramifications. It was all a paradox; absurd, contradictory scenarios that, when probed, may prove to be true. Flashbacks of the movies *Tenet* and *Millennium* continued to pop into my mind, my subconscious trying to direct me to the blindingly obvious, but it was missing a piece. Or pieces.

In my peripheral vision, I saw a shadowy figure behind me, approaching, moving way too quickly, and shortening our distance. Was it just another runner? Someone following me? The likelihood that I was targeted to be one of the next seventeen victims? I ran towards the curb to stop and bent down to tie a shoe while I scanned the horizon. A young couple in their late twenties were walking home from probably a bar, as they were laughing and swaying; another young man in a suit with a backpack, most likely a congressional aide ending his day of work; an older couple walking their labradoodle; and this mystery runner all in black. *Damn, I missed my dogs.*

He didn't slow his pace and didn't look in my direction as he ran past, but his military-grade softshell jacket gave him away. It was pretty nice, with roominess to holster firearms or a bulletproof vest, and versatile for weather conditions. The army and air force had recently changed uniforms, but this design wasn't part of our armed forces. More like Blackwater. This had all the feels of a private contractor probably hired by former specialists.

I weighed my options on how to pursue versus waiting to be pursued. Let's see how bad this knee really is, I thought, and took off to catch him.

"Call Steve," I said as I started my pursuit.

"Hola, Amiga," he answered on the first ring.

"Steve, I need you to dial in my location via satellite. I have an unknown in vicinity, and closing."

I could hear Steve typing robustly while asking me why I can't ever give him a decent heads up. Focus, Steve.

My target was gaining ground and I was at an all-out sprint to catch him, at this point, looking like the T-1000 in *Terminator 2* with arms swinging high and fast to escalate my momentum and shorten the gap. I never understood how people run with their arms looking like a T-Rex. There is some simple physics one must acknowledge; otherwise, it's counterintuitive to your efforts.

"Found you. Got your perp, too," I heard Steve exclaim.

"Can you tell which direction he's aiming?"

"He just turned left onto 15th which will head straight to FBI building, at this rate."

"Expand out. Anyone else look connected?"

"Pick up your pace, there're two unidentified males behind you – could be nothing, but they are roughly 25 yards out and closing in."

"Steve, listen closely. I'll be fine, but the guys following me are about to have a problem. Contact local assets on my command, run thru facial recognition, and stay on me," I said, out of breath.

I was coming up to 15th Street and was taking a hard turn left when my knee gave out. Fucking turns. The thrust propelled me seven feet from my location before I dropped and rolled, taking brutal force on my elbows to avoid damage to my head and face.

Intuitively, I grabbed my Spyderco Paramilitary 2 folding knife while rolling before I heard, "Baker, stop. We've been sent here on direct orders…from the President."

FIFTEEN

3.2.1. I POPPED UP LIKE JACKIE CHAN in a fighting stance, wishing I had the Rods of God capability just now. Sadly, I did not.

We were both calculating next moves. The fact that they didn't shoot me dead had me feeling a little optimistic. For the moment.

"Miss Baker. We have a secure line and have been asked to bring you in at the request of the President," they said as they handed over a phone to me.

The President? Adams?

"Matti, don't kill my guys, here. They are on 'our' team and are there on my request," I heard the President say.

WTF? This wasn't acting-president Adams. It was THE President…from the dead.

"Pardon me, Mr. President. I was under the mis-information, just like the rest of the American public, that you had passed."

"Took a clue from you. Playing possum has its benefits. Unlike in the movie *Dave*, it's my intention to have us all resurrect when the time is right."

You must appreciate any person who is so well versed in movies.

"Mr. President are you familiar with *Ready to Go* by Republica?...*Baby, I'm ready to go, I'm back, I'm ready to go. From the rooftops, shout it out…*

"Can't say I know that one," he laughed genuinely. "These gentlemen will escort you to my location. See you in a few, Matti."

In a few? Hmm. "I serve at the pleasure of the President." He had a nice chuckle on that as he hung up. It's just a matter of time before cancel culture changes that line, too. Good grief.

I initially assumed we would be heading towards the FBI Headquarters building. My mother's short-lived career was with the FBI. She 'died' immediately after childbirth with me and my two sibling brothers. Her death was self-inflicted to deter any replication of the DNA sequencing that was administered to her and, more importantly, which had created the three of us.

Outside of not meeting the age and gender requirements when I applied for my own training, I never truly considered the FBI. I found it unsettling that their Top Ten Most Wanted included pics of a 165-lb male that killed his wife in a donut shop, from five years ago.

On the plus side, the FBI was the only agency that we did not have confirmation of being compromised with any participation or associations with the other parties we were investigating.

I had previously reached out to FBI Director Coles, as the FBI is the owner of CODIS. CODIS is the Combined DNA Index System, which houses all criminal DNA and is used as a tool to aid federal, state, and local crime labs in comparing and matching DNA profiles. It was already a security concern before, but now, with China accelerating their efforts to obtain DNA profiles, it was imperative that this information did not get into the wrong hands. The previous Director of National Intelligence, who the FBI reports to, was the whore that shot Freddy and detonated us both. I barely survived. She didn't. Karma's a bitch.

I was in a black Cadillac Escalade with illegal tint and a divider partition, heading south on I-95. My escorts weren't much for talking, and kindly requested my phone prior to me entering the vehicle.

Luckily, they mistook my custom Patek Phillippe as a regular mechanical watch, and I was able to silently ping Tom to let him know I was ok. I knew Steve had heard the whole conversation and would be updating Tom and the team while monitoring, recording, and tracking my location.

Thirty minutes into the drive, I tapped on the divider and inquired how much longer. The driver stated that we were fifteen minutes out. So, we were heading to the FBI, just not headquarters, but to the Academy. The FBI Academy is located in Quantico, Virginia, with over 547 acres. More than enough space to hide the President and any team he had.

It was now almost midnight as we rolled onto the campus. The Academy programs included firearms, TEVOC (Tactical and Emergency Vehicle Operations), survival, a law enforcement executive development, and a training complex for new FBI and DEA agents to learn techniques and defensive tactics.

Maybe when I hit retirement age, this wouldn't be a bad place for me to teach others? Not like when Maverick returns after only one mission to teach the best of the best in *Top Gun*. Really? I mean, come on.

Driving up, the main training complex is the university background with dormitory buildings, a library, auditorium, training facility, gym, and administrative offices. They also have their own mock city for new agent training, with defensive driving track and firearms ranges. Now, remember what I told you about the layout of the Denver International Airport? There's a lot of room on 547 acres that haven't been accounted for.

The driver pulled over as we rolled into the entrance and handed me a head covering that he requested I put on. I was incredulous, but obliged. They needed to do this for preemptive consideration in the untimely event of my capture. We drove for another ten minutes as we weaved through the road, and I sensed the car going downward in the terrain. I heard a large mechanical door opening and closing as we entered before we finally stopped.

I was instructed to take off the head covering, and opened the door to an entourage, with one man looming larger than the others.

"Good to see you again, Matti," he said as he extended his hand.

"You too, Possum. I mean, Mr. President."

SIXTEEN

THE "BUNKER" THAT WE WERE IN made the one in *Independence Day* look like a relic. I can only imagine how much money was funneled into this. Again, it explains the invoices for the five-thousand-dollar toilet seats in the Pentagon. I mean, wow. This place was impressive.

What didn't compute was how acting President Adams didn't know that the real President was (1) alive and (2) hiding out here. Granted, she had a few things on her current plate: pandemic, vaccine, Chinese, Russia, immigration, bailouts, and a controversial election, but someone or some department from the government should have sent up some red flags. To be able to keep the President and Vice-Pres under wraps for six weeks was a monumental task, and a reminder to all that nothing is ever what it seems. NOTHING.

I was escorted, with the President, to a conference room that had all the bells and whistles. There must have been at least a hundred monitors with activity from all over the globe. Food and beverage buffets were set up and the President indicated for me to grab something prior to us taking a seat while he stepped out to attend to some quick business. I was famished, and quickly indulged.

"It appears you're keeping late hours, these days." I started speaking while he made his way in. I took another bite from a wagyu burger and chipotle curly fries. My eyes stayed on him the whole time, observing his mannerisms.

"As you've experienced, this is the witching hour where the real actions take place."

"Care to catch me up? I think we can start with your "death" and skip over the beginning."

"Impressive you could get that out with your mouth that full," he teased. "I'll spare you the long version for another time. Suffice it to say, we had internal individuals and agencies that were collaborating…well, for the simplest of explanations, Sinicization. Are you familiar with that term?"

"You mean, to modify by Chinese influence?"

"Exactly. China supplied the virus, thinking they'd take over the global economy and eventually buy our tremendous debt. They had help from multiple sources internally and internationally, creating a bloodletting effect. The VP and I were standing in their way. When they made an unsuccessful assassination attempt on our lives, we decided to take advantage of the situation to flesh out who was involved internally."

"So, that's why you had me on Wagner. You knew or suspected his connection with Adams, and she quickly reared her ugly head as the front runner."

"We suspected, but couldn't confirm until after our demise."

"Well, you had me on this "project" way before the virus hit, so congratulations on your team's prophetic skills."

"We need your and your team's assistance to bring our resurrection to fruition and our nation back to order."

"Why me?"

"You have a particular skill set. Skills you acquired over a long career; skills that make you a nightmare for people like them."

"Sweet Jesus, you are quoting *Taken*. You've really been in this bunker too long."

His smile was mischievous, but genuine. I trusted this man, but more importantly, I respected him. He wasn't letting a political party rule him, but was risking everything to protect our nation.

"We made the vaccines with help of Russia to distribute to everyone and every country but China. China believes they have successfully copied this version, as they are notorious for stealing intellectual and property rights."

"So, this inoculation is to protect all of us from the next version they try to administer?"

"Possibly, or the next version already administered…" he trailed off to leave the sinister implication.

Oh, shit. The enemy of our enemy is our newest friend.

"How can you trust the Russians on this?"

"We mutually understood it was in our best interest to contain the virus. At least, for now. Keeps us both accountable. With options."

"What, exactly, are you wanting from me and/or my team?"

"We need a Vince Papale."

We talked for another hour, probing back and forth. He had a senior officer enter to discuss and assist with some logistical preparations. It was in the wee hours of the early morning, and I was starting to show signs of sagging.

"Matti, we'll supply whatever you need, if we can. We are counting on your team to help bring this to a conclusion."

"I was already in it. Let me ask you one last thing before I have your guys take me back to my hotel. Who organized your "departure"?

He hesitated. God dammit. I already knew the answer before I asked.

Based on my reaction, he knew I now knew, too. "I instructed Freddy not to share with you or your team - for your protection."

"For our protection? That's ironic, as all of you are relying on me, now, for *your* protection," I said with a wink.

"Don't be too hard on him; he loves you more than you'll ever know."

"Save the flattery. Wait until we pull off this miracle."

Freddy had been backdooring it, all this time. I'd have to re-evaluate, as he surely wasn't slipping in his old age.

SEVENTEEN

I MADE CALLS TO TOM AND MY TEAM as the drivers escorted me back to my hotel. It was now almost 6AM and I was running on fumes. It should have been my first call, but I saved it for my last, to contact Freddy. He picked up on the first ring.

"It's 4AM, my time. Do you do this on purpose?" was how he answered the call, sounding very alert...in fact, too alert. He had been given a heads up.

"Well...Doc Holiday...In vino veritas."

"I wasn't quite as sick as I made out," he offered meekly.

"You're no daisy...yet..."

Freddy had an awkward laugh, knowing that we couldn't continue with movie quotes to express our fears and frustrations. I mean, *Tombstone* sets the bar pretty high.

"Freddy, I don't know how much clearer I can make this. It is not your responsibility to shield me for my protection. In fact, you are endangering my life and, more importantly, my family's, by not divulging the truth. Get your priorities straight, old man. You know I'm not tolerant when it comes to my family or the team."

"I was working on a bigger picture, Matti. Based on your specific DNA genetic makeup, we don't know if this virus could have a different outcome on you. For the President and our nation, I was simply facilitating a fail-safe solution."

"And all this time I was just thinking you were going for strategic incompetence. You didn't happen to pen that "Manual of Trickery and Deception," by any chance?" I inquired sarcastically.

During the 1970s, the CIA had this manual that was believed to be destroyed. The CIA brought in a magician to help agents perform magic tricks and even develop a secret language. I felt like Freddy had been using this against me my entire lifetime.

"Can't say I authored that one, but I may have been an advisor," he said, more lightheartedly. "You ready for this?"

"You mean, am I ready for the O.K. Corral?

"Timing will be crucial for success."

I simply recited "*God help the beast in me, The beast in me has had to learn to live with pain, and how to shelter from the rain, and in the twinkling of an eye, might have to be restrained...*"

"You ok, Matti? You're quoting *Sopranos*, not your usual *Tombstone.*"

"I thought you'd enjoy *God Help the Beast in Me* by Nick Lowe. Sometimes you have to combine the best with the best."

"Johnny Cash originally sang it, but I get your point."

"I'll be coming in on a commercial flight this evening, to gather the team. Be ready. And, Freddy, no more holding back. For your protection." With that nugget, I hung up and fell fast asleep.

EIGHTEEN

I AWOKE SIX HOURS LATER, feeling drugged. A fitful sleep resulted as I mentally calculated outcomes and possibilities. I called Bes and Lili and strategized with them. Tom had already forwarded to them the schematics of building plans. The wheels were in motion.

I was returning to Texas to meet up with the team before we dispersed. Each of us had a target and role in bringing this to successful fruition. Failure was not an option.

I called the kids to catch up with them, but just needed to hear their voices to calm my mind before we headed down this dangerous path. All three complained that Ainsworth was harder on them then the rest of the class. I reminded them it was because they could take it, and they must persevere. Just hearing their voices made me reminisce about the last time we were all together with the dogs.

Damn, I miss those dogs. The kids, too, but the dogs were my other babies. I just hoped Tom and/or Bethany were taking all of them out for training and rehab, for Scout. Scout, the slightly overweight red lab (ok, more than slightly, but no need to body shame) tore his ACL while playing with Koda and Bruiser. A twelve-week recovery time, and we were in week 4. Trooper, the white lab, was getting jealous from all the attention. If only you could explain things to dogs.

I felt peaceful after talking with the kids, and packed my bags to head to Ronald Reagan. It had been a hot minute since I flew commercial. *Bless my heart.* Travel restrictions were still in place due to the virus, but capacity was only marginally lower than normal. I was in 3C on a Boeing 737. I felt like it was the original 737 that was introduced in 1968, as it didn't appear to have been updated since.

Ol' *Rain Man* wouldn't be caught dead on this flight. Remember that movie? Raymond Bobbitt would only fly Qantas, as it never crashed. (Well, that airline did suffer fatal crashes prior to 1951, another movie faux pas, but was still the safest option, with no fatalities in last seventy years.) Too bad I was on American.

I was walking towards terminal C when a fellow male passenger caught my eye. His backpack was significantly larger and clearly oversized for the upper bins or under the seat. The flight attendant didn't look or even question its size as he boarded the plane. Lazy? Incompetent? Orchestrated?

Tom generally commented that I had an over-active imagination. I discarded these comments, most of the time. My experiences taught me over and over again to trust my instincts. There's a difference between profiling and stereotyping, but there's an underlying and undeniable truth to both. Just saying. Passengers and staff were all now mandated to wear masks, so subtle facial expressions were hidden. This only heightened my senses and concerns.

My fellow passenger was in 1A. I had a clear sight of him from my seat. The seat beside him was empty. Hmm. The flight was relatively full, yet here this first- class seat was open. I paid two grand for a last-minute, one way. This patron didn't look like he had two nickels to rub together.

He had his backpack somewhat under the front seat while taking up the aisle space in front of the seat beside him. Again, the flight attendant said nothing. The prickly hairs on my neck were standing up. Flights can't give you drinks or food, due to virus concerns, so I don't know...do your job. Just a thought.

The pilot got on the loudspeaker and dribbled on about how the flight would be over in three and a half hours, updated us on the weather conditions, and apologized that the Wi-Fi was out. I'd be fine just sleeping for the duration, but knew that sleep would elude me as long as this fellow passenger continued his disconcerting actions.

I had some heavy reading material to get through, courtesy of the Pres, and I'd also picked up an indie book in the terminal, a paranormal Celtic romance. Not my normal reading genre, but hey, why not. I opted to start the flight with the indie book. I quickly texted Tom and the kids our customary "Lo" text, to signify that the flight was taking off.

There are two types of passengers on planes – the kind who can't sleep, or the ones who nod off immediately at takeoff. I fall into the second category. Normally. Aircrafts are pressurized to six thousand to eight thousand feet above sea level. At the higher altitude, your blood absorbs less oxygen, which makes you tired. Combine this with the force of takeoff, and it impersonates the perception of lying down. Couple this with the white noise of the engines and the dimming of lights and you can call it an optimal lights-out scenario.

My eyes felt more tired than usual. The gaiter I was using for a mask was suffocating and confining. Before the plane even leveled off, I unbuckled my seat belt and went to the restroom to splash some water on my face to wake me up. I motioned to the flight attendants, like I was about to get sick. I just sat in there for over twenty minutes as I continued to run water up and down my arms and face – anything to keep me awake. My eyes were irritated and red. Probably just dehydration. Reluctantly, I pulled the gaiter back over my face to return.

When I finally opened the door to return to my seat, Passenger 1A was no longer there. Neither was the backpack. All passengers appeared to be in a deep slumber. *Oh, shit – that doesn't compute well.* The one area that does not have ventilation blowing in a plane is the bathroom. It may have just saved my life. I quickly lowered my body closer to the ground as I saw the gases emitting from the vents and made my way the attendant's closet to grab an oxygen mask. I grabbed the portable oxygen bottle and took several deep breaths as I secured it on my face. I hurriedly returned to check the pulse on the passenger in 3D. There was none. *MOTHER FUCKER.*

I looked down the aisles to the other passengers, who were "asleep" as well, and saw a flight attendant face down on the floor. *MOTHER….* I could deduct that the pilots were impacted, as well. That wasn't an ordinary backpack, but most likely a parachute, as this was a suicide mission with no intention to have any survivors. Either that, or it held explosives. Thus, another reason for my lack of trust issues with TSA pre-screening.

I had to find Passenger 1A while simultaneously potentially flying and landing this plane. I stayed near to the ground to stay out of sight and grabbed the closest flight attendant's key card and opened up the cockpit. Just as I had anticipated, both pilots had no pulse. Luckily, the plane was on autopilot. I had a small window of time, now, to locate the perp.

What were odds that this was a random act of terrorism? Was I the main target? Did he assume I'd return to my seat quickly and thus suffer the same fate as the others? Besides my team, who else knew I was on this flight? Who else was on this flight who could be targeted? Did the passenger check-in flight attendant willingly know and participate?

Luckily for me, these pilots originated from Texas. God Bless Texas. After 9/11, the Arming Pilots Against Terrorism Act was passed, allowing pilots the option to carry guns in the cockpit. Our Texas boys had a Beretta M9 with extra clips in the cockpit. Time to put it to good use.

I scanned the controls to see if there was anything indicating the whereabouts of 1A. *Think.* Unless his mission was to go down with the plane (which was highly possible), he had to get off it without bringing attention to his departure when officials went through the wreckage. The 737 was designed not to have landing gear doors, as there wasn't enough space to open them under the craft to accommodate them, as the plane was designed to be low to the ground. A manual extension would be possible with the landing gear in any position, but…there's always a but…the optimal height to parachute out would be at ten thousand feet.

We were presently cruising at thirty-five thousand feet. Thus, the reason why airlines don't carry parachutes for passengers. Special team forces are trained to jump at higher altitudes, but they are specially trained, and have special equipment. 1A didn't appear to be in that category. He'd have to lower the plane to get back lower to jump, which meant that he'd have to return to the cockpit and take it off autopilot.

I could dump fuel to speed up this next transaction, but we weren't flying over a body of water, like *Captain Sully* or the scene in *Air Force One*, and although I considered myself proficient at aerodynamics, I wasn't at the caliber of Bethany. So, my option was handed to me, to wait for 1A to return to the cockpit.

Now, if I was going to stage a plane going down, I'd do it within the first thirty minutes of the flight taking off. Not for any reason someone else may be thinking of, but just the sheer fact that I'd want to get it over with.

I slowly and carefully maneuvered to row 7B – the first row after first class. If 1A was planning my demise, he'd notice I wasn't there. If I happen to be 'coincidental' carnage, then he wouldn't be looking for or suspecting me in 7B, as all other passengers were no longer with us. I grabbed the passenger's scarf beside me to conceal my oxygen mask and tilted my face down into my chest while keeping my eyes slightly open. I had less than twenty minutes remaining on this mask. Tick tock.

Trust me, it's harder than you think to not move…at all. I thought about Tom, the kids, Freddy, Bethany, and the boys. I could not let this be my ending. I would not let it be. I said a silent prayer.

Finally, I heard movement at the rear of the plane. He was making his way up. I had less than five minutes remaining on my oxygen. *For the Love of God, hurry the f up.* It sounded like he was checking on certain passengers. Possibly to identify them, or possibly to just make sure they were deceased. I estimated there were over one hundred fifty passengers and crew on this flying coffin.

Three minutes remaining.

Since I was unable to turn or react, I closed my eyes and just listened. Phil Collins', *I Don't Care Anymore* simultaneously ran through my thoughts… *And as for me, I can sit here and bide my time, I got nothing to lose if I speak my mind, I don't care anymore…*

Two minutes, forty-five seconds remaining. Dammit.

He was getting closer. I could feel him approaching. What the fuck was he waiting on, or doing? Then I heard it. He was talking to someone. It sounded like he was using an old-time transmitter. I was unfamiliar with the language he spoke, and I've traveled the world and know quite a few. The other person came off barking, sounding agitated. More importantly, the other person was a female. The transmission stopped.

Two minutes fifteen.

He passed me, luckily not giving me any notice, but rapidly turned a one eighty when he noticed that no one was in seat 3B. His tank was in front of him, shielding his torso. Dammit. He scanned the room with an AK-47 pointed at the dead passengers. I'm sure he deliberated that he couldn't shoot off 45 rounds giving notice of his true intentions when this plane crashed. He lowered his weapon momentarily as he pondered his next action.

Big mistake. Huge. I popped up and aimed the Beretta at his head. I couldn't chance hitting his chest and exploding the both of us. His brown, beady eyes narrowed on my location. He wasn't coming out of this alive, despite me needing information from him. He understood that it was a showdown. *Fat chance, loser.* His eyes grew wide, then he smiled demonically as he attempted to level his AK.

You can't reason with crazy, nor should you try. I cocked my head as I pulled the trigger, saying, "Mors Tua Vita Mea."

Matthew McConaughey said it best in *The Gentlemen… If you wish to be The King of the jungle, it's not enough to act like a king. You must be The King. And there can be no doubt. Because doubt causes chaos and one's own demise…*

NINETEEN

I HAD UNDER TWO MINUTES OF AIR remaining and ran. I felt like Nic Cage in *Face-Off,* where he had seconds to shut off the device he'd planted. Unlike his scenario, I still had to locate the dilemma, determine how to dismantle it, and try not to suffocate and die while doing so. *Easy-peasy.*

Pressurized air in planes is a result of fresh air from outside coming in and recirculating through HEPA filters, which remove microscopic levels of bacteria and clusters. These filters are 99.9 effective in removing unwanted microscopic sources. Despite the public's concern with air flying and virus contamination, it really is one of the safer situations to be in. These filters allow air to recirculate in the cabin every two to three minutes. I was counting on finding my quarry here. And I did. Bingo. *Thank God.*

After locating the source of contamination in the HEPA filters and carefully removing it, the ventilation system would be back to fully operational. I used the oxygen masks below until I could verify the new readings with an all clear, and then headed back to the cockpit. I managed to open comms and contacted Bethany directly.

"B, we have a situation. Dial in the team, we're going to need all hands-on board."

"What is it this time?"

"Going to need to keep off FAA radar for time being, and terminate this 737. The passengers and crew are all dead, so we'll need to collaborate on that, as well."

"Funny, stop dinking on the plane."

"Wish I was, B. Get the team together."

"Oh, fuuuuuuck."

The team assembled, and Freddy was first to address me. "What the hell happened, Matti?"

"I was hoping you might have more intel on this, but keeping it short for time being for self-preservation, someone was trying to take me out and make it look like an airplane malfunction."

"We may just have to follow through on that. This is too big to cover up with no time."

"Already thought about that option. How big is that lake in Grapevine, Texas?"

We strategized for roughly thirty minutes. This plane had already passed Memphis and was now over the Arkansas border. I could maintain autopilot until Texarkana when the FAA would most likely contact or an update. That didn't provide us much time. Steve had backdoored and tied our comms to theirs. We'd find out quickly how well Jake and Tom could improv as the original pilots and navigate conversation through an unrecoverable engine failure. It needed to be recorded for the black box they'd locate at the bottom of the lake. Bethany would be instructing me how to pilot accordingly, and then remotely, as I used 1A's pack to perform the jump he'd never made. Freddy would be working locally at the lake and airport to manufacture a reason to clear a path, but the lake should be vacant due to late evening time.

It wasn't the best plan, but it was only option we had, at the moment. We all agreed, and disbursed to get ready. Tom requested that I stay online for a private moment.

"It's just us. You ok?" he asked, concerned.

"I'm just so tired, Tom. When does it ever end?"

"I know, babe. You just have to keep at the forefront that your efforts now will impact and help millions of other people. Possibly billions."

"And these hundred and fifty that had to die because of me, and our efforts to contain this?" I continued with my voice cracking. "Their families will be notified of their tragic, horrific deaths. The continued vile manipulation of others will impact them forever. It's this shit that eats at me…to the core."

"Matti, you didn't start this. Those families are counting on you to end this. The public will know the truth, eventually."

I didn't have the heart to correct him. They wouldn't know any truth in their lifetime to give them any relief, perspective, or closure. I wish I was still as naïve as he was, on these matters.

"I hope so. Thanks, babe. I love you. You need to get ready. We're counting on your pristine acting skills to pull this off."

"I'll create my IMBD profile right after. Maybe we can start a new gig after this is all done?" he offered solemnly, but teasingly, to lighten the mood.

"Probably shouldn't post that pic with your readers on in your bio."

"Lock it up. You never miss a beat, Matti. Love you, babe. I'll see you in a few."

I grabbed the gear and walked the aisle, repeating the hymnal…*I vow to thee my country, all earthly things above, Entire and whole and perfect, the service of my love; The love that asks no questions, the love that stands the test, That lays upon the altar, the dearest and the best...*

Airlines coming into DFW airport from the north entrance must go over Grapevine Lake to arrive at the terminals. It's situated just twenty miles northwest and has roughly eight thousand acres. We were aiming for a three-mile stretch in the lake that did not house ramps, boat access, and should have no traffic due to nighttime hours.

Jake and Steve were contacted by FAA about high winds and instructed to come in from north, versus the original flight plan to enter from the south. The manufactured static on the line was the perfect cover, and so far, they were handling things incredibly. An Oscar-worthy performance. No one was the wiser, and fortunate for us, no one in the tower knew these pilots personally. We needed all the help we could get.

My window would be small, as the FAA would be notified when the landing gear was activated. We implanted a delayed response, basically a virus, in their system. It takes a plane on average thirty minutes to descend, but the minimum time is ten minutes. Our decreased cruising altitude would be in line with the descent.

I had previously inspected the pack, and luckily, 1A had the two-chute equipment that must be certified and licensed by none other than the FAA. Whether it's your first jump or your thousandth, skydivers were required to have two parachutes, per FAA regulations. I carefully modified this one to use only one. The other was the cover for our "malfunction." After going through the few remains of 1A and taking pictures, I moved him into position to "jump" with me.

Dark in the cockpit, Bethany was now instructing me on the display panel. Twist this, turn this, pull this lever…and viola, she now had complete control of the airplane remotely, and was in position to bring it down.

"Get down below. I have controls. You'll have roughly thirty seconds to dump and clear after I give you the 'Go'."

"What could go wrong?" I professed.

"Plenty – you better take the Air Force's motto to heart and Aim High."

"Fly, Fight, Win – got it. Let's do this."

Once in position, I waited patiently for the command with 1A in front of me. With limited night visibility and without any preferred equipment, I was going off blind faith. I did manage to locate a handheld flashlight, hoping that would suffice to give me enough notice to steer clear and not hit the wing, a tree, a house, or something worse.

"In position B."

"You got this, Matti. On my mark, in 3-2-1."

With that, I stepped off with 1A to reach terminal velocity. Bethany navigated the plane to veer left while I simultaneously projected 1A to the right engine. I pulled the ripcord of my chute to slow my resistance over the plane and soon-to-be wreckage. 1A hit squarely in the engine, engulfing him immediately and providing the desired impact. Like flying through a flock of seagulls, the irrecoverable malfunction would be cited as being due to a night skydive gone wrong. His mangled body parts would be unrecognizable, and fish food for Grapevine Lake.

I glided over towards the north side. The cool evening with its full moon and stars delivered more than ample light to guide me effortlessly, and would have been heavenly had I not witnessed the engulfing flames of death with no one screaming but my silent own.

Save Yourself by Stabbing Westward haunted my thoughts… *I know that you've been damaged, your soul has suffered such abuse, but I am not your savior, I am just as fucked as you…*

TWENTY

Texas

FREDDY WAS IN THE VICINITY as he tracked me gliding effortlessly down. I reflected on Doug during my decent. I prayed my landing would stick easily, so not to further injure my knee. I was grateful that no kids were around the lake partying, avoiding supplementary attention. Touchdown uneventful, I packed the rig while I waited for Freddy to arrive at my location.

He pulled up, driving my baby, my Jag C-X75. Just so wrong.

"Figured you haven't driven this in a while, and it needed to be recharged."

"Little flashy for this particular occasion, don't you think?"

"True. My Suburban would have been better. Also figured you could use a little pick-me-up."

"Then you should have brought the dogs. Move over. Don't even think you're driving."

Twenty minutes later, we arrived at the house and the gang came out and greeted me, including all four dogs. I was grateful to be with them all. It was an unspoken rule: we hugged, patted each other backs, and then just moved on, for the time being. A *Sons of Anarchy* moment. I informed them I needed to shower and refresh and told them to meet in the conference room in an hour, to go over next steps. No time for the weary.

Holding my hand, Tom steered me towards the steam shower and turned it on while he went to grab some fresh towels. I walked in fully clothed and plopped down on the floor. When he saw me, he entered and joined me. It was the same scene as *Casino Royale* with Daniel Craig and Eva Green, but unlike the movie, Tom unclothed me to pull me into a full embrace. Nothing more needed to be said.

Once put together, I walked into our secure conference room where everyone was already situated. Bethany had arranged an amuse-gueule assortment and had decanted some Biondi Santi Brunello, a delicious Italian Tuscan.

"Steve, where are we on the identity of 1A?"

"He's Mongolian. Name: Batzorig. They don't normally have surname; they follow with patronymic origin. Has a history of involvement in various terrorist organizations, but is considered a minor player."

"And the transmitter? Can we determine who/where he was communicating with?"

"Still working on that, but we can confirm that the last transmission was within the DC area."

"Looks like we need to revisit our Bureau Chief Davidson. Where are Wagner and Wilson now?"

The gang looked anxiously around, waiting to see who would speak up first.

I looked around and laid my eyes toward the one momentarily most invested in it. "Spill it, Jake."

"Wagner is in the extra guest house. We set up a *9 to 5* scenario. Consider him Dabney Coleman, at the moment."

"And Wilson?"

He shifted in his seat. The tension in the room just rocketed amongst the group. "Despite others' input, I have her in the room I'm occupying. She is restrained, too, just so you know."

"Good grief. I bet she is." I was too tired at the moment to fight about the poor choice, and looked towards the others to indicate my displeasure that they'd conceded with this decision. They looked away like admonished children.

"We'll deal with that issue when the time comes. For now, let's focus on next steps and drill down on what needs to be done. Someone just tried to blow me out of the sky and took out one hundred fifty innocent human beings. Let's focus."

"Well, technically, one-fifty-one, including Batzorig."

"Steve, I swear to Christ, you may make it one-fifty-two."

"My bad. Apologies…too soon."

I looked over to Bethany, who didn't look back.

TWENTY-ONE

OPERATION MEDUSA WAS FORMULATED at the drawing board. In Greek mythology, Medusa was one of three sisters, and had venomous snakes in place of hair. Those who gazed into her eyes could still be turned into stone even after her beheading. We'd be doing the beheading, this time.

While we tackled China, Russia, and ourselves internally, we needed to simultaneously take off the heads of all three, while concealing the repercussions to ensure that the public was shielded from further influences. Coordinating time attacks in different time zones and countries concurrently is no small feat. Plus, they would be after me, still.

We would be unable to utilize the full resources of our missing-in-action President, nor our friends at the FBI, until 'the awakening'. There was the all too familiar concept that if anything went wrong, individuals and our actions would be denied any knowledge or affiliation. The lyrics of Bolt Thrower, *No Guts, No Glory,* rang ever true… *The last advance, one final chance, it now shall be, no guts, no glory…* The actual origination of the phrase is credited to Air Force Major General Frederick Corbin in 1955, who wrote a manual about air-to-air combat. I had my own idea of a manual to write after this mission (aka Shitshow).

"Matti, don't you think we need to first address how they know you were on that plane? And, more importantly, why would they sacrifice the entire plane?"

Freddy interjected, "The answer to the latter is plausible deniability. In terms of how they tracked her, I have two guesses on that. Either Davidson had her trailed the whole time, or, Steve, tap in really quick and see who has reported any cyber-attack breaches."

Steve banged away on the keyboard while the rest of us discussed (argued) over next steps.

Finally, he printed off a recent list of hacks and brought it over to me. My eyes closed and I had an immediate disgusted look on my face as I took a deep breath in. "Well, Freddy, care to explain to the team why you had Steve run that?"

"I figured Davidson might be checking out more than your ass when you met up. Can't expect the Bureau Chief of Homeland Security not to notice your custom watch."

"Wait, back up. What's this about Davidson?" piqued Bethany with a smirk.

"She was a little touchy," I blandly offered.

"Pray tell," added Tom with a chuckle and a wink.

"Stop, you whore mongers. It was nothing. We need to focus."

"Notice that Matti is great at deflecting when it comes to the fun stuff," chided Jake.

"If she tapped into Patek, then she also knows our whereabouts now, and that I didn't go down with the plane. We need to prepare for the arsenal she'll send. If they had no qualms taking out a plane, a few acres will be nothing."

Collectively, the team considered and thought…*Fuuudge.*

Freddy looked at me with that knowing look. He nodded towards me, then said, "It's your rodeo. How do you want to proceed?"

"Jake, Steve – head to the supply room. We're going to set up a *Home Alone* scenario. Bethany, grab the gear and prep the plane. Freddy, you and Tom need to take off and locate us a new base camp, pronto, with our 'guests', and coordinate with B for the next steps. Take Scout and Trooper with you, too. Tom, you also need to reach out to our favorite realtor, as we'll be relocating. Looks like we're about to give her some new business again. Let's identify some place cooler than this hundred-plus-degree Texas heat. I need to get in touch with Bes and Lily and fill them in. We don't know how much time we have, so get cracking. America needs their favorite team to win this Super Bowl."

"The Cowboys haven't won since 1996," Steve responded, deadpan.

I glanced over to Bethany. "You must be so proud."

She nervously laughed.

"Ok, let's get moving."

TWENTY-TWO

BES AND LILY HAD ALREADY STARTED arrangements for the next steps. Lily was not in favor with the direction we were taking, and was vocal about it. Bes understood the short- and long-term ramifications, but had doubts about our ability to pull this off, with as many parameters we had in play.

"I don't know what the difference is between killing them and taking them hostage," she contended.

"We've discussed this ad nauseum, Lily. We don't even know how far the breach is, but it's larger than we can contain in the amount of time we are allotted. Don't worry, they will all get their due justice."

"Justice would be them dead."

"Bes, help me out here," I pleaded.

"She scares me even more than you."

Fair point. "Lily, we're out of time. We need to proceed, and we can readdress a new direction after the announcements."

"For the record, I'd like it noted that I was not in favor."

"Noted. Ok, are you both ready on what you need and when?"

"I was born ready," Lily added.

Holy shit.

Unlike the previous time when we made trenches around my house to take out our enemies, we did not have the time to replicate, but made other preparations. Trenches have played a significant role in military history, dating back to WWI. Trenches were used to counteract the use of artillery, thus that's why they had sharp angles, zigged, and curved to diffuse and minimize the explosive shrapnel from artillery impact. We also didn't have time for barbed wire, machine gun nests, or dugouts.

Military tactics have changed exponentially since WWI. War was almost considered romantic, back then. The French wore blue uniforms with white gloves. They might as well have said, "Hey, we are here! *Kill us now.*" Soldiers didn't understand that war was hell. Horses and animals played a huge part, as well, in previous wars.

Oftentimes, you must look back to see where you need to go. We'd have to intertwine a bit from the past with the future, to be successful.

More importantly, with the advancement of technology, our adversaries most likely would be using Smart Goggles and iVests, which had augmented human infantry taking it to the next level. A 3-D holographic map of our entire team would be used for an entirely new way to kill. It also provided them knowledge of how many rounds in your weapon versus theirs, with GPS points for rapid target acquisition which could even shoot around corners. Hell, this new warfare technology even monitors your health. The hardest hurdle was how to implement this without overwhelming the soldier. Unlike in *Terminator*, the human brain can only process so much, and we would need to misdirect humans and technology.

With limited time, we were setting up robotic mannequins to mimic our movements from two hundred yards out. We would be using the same technology to locate our foes on the reverse end. Completely covered from head to toe in heat-reducing gear, they couldn't even see the white of our eyes. We looked like our own version of *Predator*.

This Texas heat was a killer, and we would be limited in the amount of time before dehydration symptoms affected our abilities. Koda and Bruiser would be aiding in our efforts, as their natural roaming movements and surveillance would be monitored by the enemy, as well.

The worst part would be the waiting. Would they come immediately? Wait until nightfall? So, we decided they needed a little push, and I texted our pal Davidson with just two words:

YOU MISSED

I reluctantly took off my Patek and placed it on the mannequin, then looked at the boys and told them to take their places, with a reminder to go to the new channel, from here. I put on a new personalized modified Chopard watch that combined luxury with tactical innovation. It was pretty sweet, if I do say so myself.

Jake offered, "What song are we going with?"

"I was thinking *Ready to Go by Republica*," Steve suggested.

"Steve, that's about the first smart thing you've said in a while. I agree." *How apropos since I'd just suggested this to the Prez. Despite it all, I loved this knucklehead.* And then we left in opposite directions, silently humming to… *I'm standing on the rooftops shouting out - Baby, I'm ready to go. I'm back, I'm ready to go…*

One hour became two, three, and then four. *Damn, it's hot.* Jake and Steve were navigating movement in the house while I was monitoring the land and sky for planes, drones, and anything that moved. The whole time, we were talking to each other as if we were still in the house. They'd be listening. *Fuck, it's hot. Maybe we should move back to Montana.* Sweat was pouring from our bodies, and we needed to limit our heat exposure. Nighttime was finally falling on us, and, thankfully, would help with this unbearable heat.

Koda and Bruiser were on high alert and were investigating everything. Their movements assisted with the perception of reality we were trying to create.

Bruiser lifted his head and caught wind of something first. He headed ninety degrees in a northeast direction and went out on a full sprint, with Koda tracking right behind him. There was only one road that led to the residence with the entrance three miles out. We anticipated they'd be dropped off outside of there and would work their way in. I silently said a prayer, asking to give me discernment and the persistence to kill anyone that messed with my dogs. Let the Lord have mercy on them. They'd need it, if they hurt my dogs. I wouldn't give it to them.

Freddy was monitoring from a secure satellite and pinged us: closing in, 6 circle.

So, they'd sent a team of six that was circling the perimeter. *That's it?!*

I looked through the scope of my JW3 TTI MPX. The accuracy and precision of this was unmatched. It sported two ten rounds, normally. I accelerated this with an add-on, making it one hundred rounds. Almost 1.5 billion shells were fired in WWI. We were ready to simulate.

Our goal was to bring them in within fifty feet of the perimeter of the main house. Koda and Bruiser returned to the house and entered through the side kitchen door, luring our new friends closer.

Just like when your phone autocorrects, AI technology projects what it shows you based on milliseconds of each picture it detects. This allows for manipulation. You see what you want to see. Technology is no different. Our targets were coming in closer to inspect.

Breathe in, breathe out.

Jake and Steve had to expertly control the mannequins with movements synced to our voices. Consider it like human *BattleBots* on steroids. If our adversary shot at one, we needed it to face plant so as not to thwart our overall game plan. We were bringing them closer anticipating they'd want to go *Narcos* on us and take us all out at once.

One hundred feet out. We needed them just a little closer.

Through my scope, I anxiously watched the movement inside, waiting to alert the dogs at the exact moment. Slowly, our adversaries flanked us, hand motioning to each other for a timed attack.

Wait for it, wait for it…Ten, nine, eight, seven – almost there, a few more feet. Three, two, one. I blew the dog whistle that our enemies would not hear. Koda and Bruiser sprinted out of the house at thirty miles per hour. At this rate, they would travel over forty-four feet per second and would pass our friends before they even knew what hit them.

Our foes reactively charged the building. The last thing they would hear would be the sound of the bullet from my rifle blazing past their ears, detonating the C4 that surrounded the main residence and continued towards the guest houses. There would be nothing left of either property or lives.

War is hell, and there is no civility anymore.

This surely takes Talking Heads' *Burning Down the House* to a new level... *Burning down the house, my house, is out of the ordinary...Burning down the house...*

The dogs approached me, excitedly licking my concealed face. "Atta boys." I looked at the carnage of the property as the flames grew higher.

I grabbed the burner phone and sent Davidson a picture of the scene and a message:

YOU'RE NEXT

TWENTY-THREE

FROM HERE ON OUT, the clock would be escalated, and we would be operating under warp speed. Adams and Davidson would be scrambling to conceal, spin the story, and get control by elimination. Of course, when you are the acting President and Bureau Chief of Homeland Security, you had considerably more resources at hand versus the average criminal.

Bethany had the plane stocked and ready for wheels up when we arrived. I'm not talking beverages, either (though there was plenty of those, too). From weaponry to communications and even disguises, we were ready for land or water. Technically, even space, too.

Freddy was escorting Wagner and Wilson to our new compound in a small town called Perry Park, between Denver and Colorado Springs. Our realtor was loving us, as she located a parcel with one hundred acres and four residences that we would be modifying. *We better get a kickass thank you gift after this purchase.* Situated between mountains, red rocks, horse farms, and man-made lakes, we found a little slice of heaven to build our next reinforced fortress.

Bonus: It was situated less than an hour and half from the kids. What can I say? Momma bear.

The rest of us were headed back to D.C. Jake had been tracking Adams and Davidson, and both were still confirmed there. We had to get there before they had any intentions of leaving. No need to incent Bethany to fly faster; her living motto was *I feel the need...the need for speed.*

Tom was coordinating with Bes and Lily and was providing them with schematics of buildings, cities, and armory deposits. I reminded them again the mission was not to kill, but to detain. No guarantee was given. I envisioned Lily wanting to march them down like the Bataan Death March. Killing them would not bring her closure. Her country was taking a massive hit due to this virus, and its future was not secure. An eye for an eye would not be enough for her.

Steve assisted me in programming 3D scans for our next project, which involved intricate and precise details down to the fingernail. While plugging away, he asked, "We ok, Matti? You've been a little hard on me lately."

Damn, he's right. "Sorry, buddy. We're good, Steve. I know I've been rough on you, lately. I just worry what happens if it doesn't work out between you and Bethany. It affects our whole team."

"Thanks for the faith," he rebuked.

Damn. "Not everyone gets the fairy tale brother. I'm just looking out for her, and the team."

"I understand, but Matti, this is my fairytale. I know what I have. I'm not letting her go. Ever. So, no need to be anxious. Trust in us...and get over it, already," he added, with a crooked smile and a wink.

Steve and Jake had saved my life on more than one occasion. From a psycho that tried to mallet my feet to when I was on a kill mat, I've counted on these boys to bring me back to life. There's a certain undeniable bond after these types of experiences. You'd gladly give your life for theirs. That's what we had.

My smile broadened as I looked at him, "Don't fuck this up. Who else am I'm going to sing bad karaoke with?"

Nothing more needed to be said. It was done. After a few moments, he added, "Matti, I know you usually talk more to Jake about personal things, but I didn't share with the others why you contacted Doug."

My eyes narrowed while I mentally calculated the probabilities. "Your surveillance on my run tipped you off?"

"Dammit, how do you always do that? Yes. When I saw you fall on that turn, I knew something was wrong. I also recalled you'd previously referred Doug to your doc, so I poked around and saw there was an appointment with Rihani that you'd made. I haven't mentioned this to anyone else. Including Tom."

Just hearing Doug's name brought a flurry of emotions: sadness, guilt, despair, and vengeance. "Thanks for your discretion, Steve. It's most likely nothing, but I didn't want to alarm anyone until I had an evaluation. I respectfully ask you continue to please keep it to yourself, for the time being."

"You don't need to worry, Matti, you're the best of the best." The twinkle in his eyes was growing.

"Killing me, smalls." *I love this dude.*

"Is this a good time to bring up an increase in our compensation?" he added with a laugh.

"You're funny, too." *I seriously question my judgment, at times.*

TWENTY-FOUR

PART OF 'OPERATION MEDUSA' included the calculation of planned obsolescence on a grander scale. You see this theory in practice in most consumer goods. Cars come out with a newer, tweaked model; ten-year lightbulbs burn out after a year; a newer version of your smartphone comes out with more memory, photo processing, speed, and of course, new accessories that you must purchase with the newer version. Your version becomes rapidly obsolete and even non-serviceable.

It's not illegal, either. The Consumer Products Safety Commission could issue standards that companies would have to adhere to, but generally they don't. Apple did get hit with a penalty when it was confirmed they'd hid battery-related problems and made a profit from selling a newer version, but what's a hundred million dollar fine, to a trillion-dollar company? Accounting error. Chump change.

For our plan to work, we needed to become prehistoric. More specifically, our objective was to approach our targets more like velociraptors. We would be coordinating our timed attacks of our enemies from the side, and would be just as vicious and cunning as the species itself. (Unlike in the movie *Jurassic Park*, most velociraptors were documented to only be the size of a turkey. Go figure.)

Tom came to the back of the plane, and we rehashed logistics and caught up on normal aspects of life. Ironic, that we were planning timed attacks while also needing to discuss what we wanted to do for a family vacation. What can I say? We're people with lives and family, too.

"I noticed you didn't jump on the bike today," he added nonchalantly. *Shit.*

"Too much going on."

"Really?" he cocked his head slightly, calling out my bullshit.

I had a little OCD complex when it came to working out on my Peloton. It helped me burn off steam while I mentally worked through assignments. Plus, ever since they added the extra non-bike workouts, I was able to change up my routine and really focus on definition. I had bikes at every residence, and even one on this plane. Listening to song remixes as instructors Dennis, Alex, or Ally pushed me to do better was just an added incentive. When I went MIA for twelve months, this was the only way I could connect with Tom while the rest of the world was trying to hunt me down and kill me. *Fuckers.* It was my happy, almost nostalgic place, so of course Tom and the others would know something was off if I wasn't working out.

Tom wrapped me up in his big strong arms while nestling my head into the crook of his broad shoulders. We stood there like that for a hot moment. He gently pulled my head back and gave me a lingering kiss before almost whispering, "I know you'll fill me in when it's necessary. Don't feel like you always have to do everything on your own, though, love."

I pulled back to look at him. He always knew what I needed or wanted. I'm not sure how many men could handle my lifestyle and situations. (Statistically, none, really.) I was indeed blessed by a higher power.

"I love you babe. All is well. Just need to work on some fine tuning. No need to worry."

"Oh, fine tuning, huh? I can help you with that right now," he said with a sexy hint.

I laughed. "Dude, we're about to land in two minutes."

"And…your point is?"

"Stop it. I'll make it up to you. I promise."

"Damn, Skippy, you better."

As Bethany was landing in D.C., you could feel the emotions of each of us heightening like the beginning crescendo of *Lose Yourself* by Eminem. Slowly, at first, then increasing, until you feel your blood flowing and fists pumping…*If you had one shot, or one opportunity. To seize everything you ever wanted, in one moment, would you capture it, or just let it slip…* We weren't in the business to let anything slip. It was time to divide and attack – velociraptor style.

I called Freddy to get a quick status update on the necessary arrangements at the compound, and confirmation on the additional intel on Chanlor. Wagner and possibly Chanlor would be escorted to their new permanent residence at the SuperMax ADX facility in the Rockies. They'd have to go to an interim place, first.

We had previously "housed" another inmate at this high-level secure penitentiary, and, interesting enough, they were able to get out with the help of some higher-level assistance. I'm not talking God, here, either. There is only one Supermax prison in the US, and if you get out, then something went terribly wrong. Of course, the public would never know or hear about this story.

All was copasetic on the home front with Freddy, and he was securing the additional intel on Chanlor via the interrogation of Wagner. I didn't ask what technique he was using, but waterboarding was a distinct possibility. Of course, he could shove ice cubes down his throat, and no one would be the wiser once it melted. If not those methods, he had the dogs he could utilize. Just saying.

Upon landing, we each had our respective roles and directives and would be splitting up immediately. Bethany and Jake would be with me as we hunted down Davidson first and then Adams. I was holding off on telling Jake anything on Chanlor until we had confirmation. He wasn't going to be happy. Steve and Tom would be coordinating efforts with Bes and Lily while taking care of provisions for next steps. We huddled together and did a quick sync on watches and timelines.

"Steve, give us a good one to head out on."

"Oh, I'm on it. *Dr. Evil* by They Might be Giants. "Interesting. From the Austin Powers movie, *The Spy Who Shagged Me*?"

"Yep...*Heaven, help you then, you're finished, it's the end. There'll be no retrieval from the Evil...*"

Breathe in, breathe out. 3.2.1. – it was go time.

TWENTY-FIVE

TO TRACK DOWN ADAMS AND DAVIDSON, we enlisted the help of our Israeli associates. Pegasus spyware was developed specifically to be covertly installed on mobile phones for reading texts, tracking calls, collecting passwords, accessing microphones, and camera and location tracking. Multiple governments have utilized this military-grade spyware to track down terrorists and criminals. Don't kid yourself: this is used on civilians, as well. Most recently, its applications have been centered on journalists, activists, and media professionals. Somewhat redundant targets if you ask me.

It was named Pegasus (more like the Trojan horse) for its ability to fly in the air to infect phones. It's the next generation of warfare and cyber security.

Bes assisted in the negotiation of this transaction, and I was sure there would be a quid pro quo request in return. We had full coverage on the whereabouts of Adams and Davidson, thanks to this new arrangement. You had the acting President and Homeland Security being breached by internal and external forces. Talk about a false sense of security. Again, reminded me of TSA at the airports. What a joke.

Adams and Davidson were in panic mode. Not only had they failed to eliminate me, but they now also understood I was coming to eliminate them. Adams had the additional task of hiding, while also needing to carry out her duties and responsibilities as the acting President. Good luck with that, Madame President.

The White House has two rooms to secure the President, in the event of an emergency or crisis. One is the Situation Room in the West Wing, for intelligence management. It's run by the NSC staff for the President and his/her advisors, including National Security and Homeland Security. This would have been the most logical choice since it would not appear out of the norm to have both Adams and Davidson present.

The other safe room in the White House is on the other side, under the East Wing. The Presidential Emergency Operations Center is a bunker-like structure with secure communications. This would be too suspicious under the present situation, unless they manifested another false security alert (which we wouldn't put past them, at this point).

Adams selected to meet Davidson at the Pentagon. The Pentagon is within fifteen minutes from the White House. Specifically, Adams instructed her to go to the National Military Command Center. This is in the Joint Staff area of the Pentagon, and held the capability to generate Emergency Action Messages and command nuclear subs, battlefield commanders and the launch control center. The room was operated by rotating teams of up to twenty personnel, led by a brigadier general or admiral.   What have I always said about reasoning with crazy? You can't. She might be bat shit crazy, but she wasn't stupid. She understood how to play the game, and had the resources at her command. Literally and figuratively.

The Pentagon building sits on twenty-nine acres, with one hundred and thirty-one stairways, nineteen escalators, and two hundred and eighty-four rest rooms. It's friggin' massive. We had a team of three to breach and secure two targets in this scenario. F'me. The only upside was that Davidson was still at her personal residence, securing items to take with her. Our window was closing.

Davidson lived in Arlington Heights Historic district, which was a stone's throw to the Pentagon. Me, personally—I wouldn't have returned to my primary residence knowing I had a highly trained operative coming for me. What did she need so badly that she had to take the calculated risk? Our bet? She had documentation to use as a bargaining chip.

We were situated down the street from Davidson's residence in a black Ford transit Connect XL cargo van with a Molly Maids cleaning logo. Bethany communicated with Davidson that Adams had arranged secure transportation to bring her to the Pentagon, and would arrive within twenty minutes with a detail from Secret Service. Meanwhile, Bethany sent Adams a secure message stating that Davidson would arrive within thirty, and two members of Secret Service would be facilitating her entrance to Command Center. Neither would be suspicious, as Secret Service operates under control of Homeland Security. Jake assisted me in prepping my disguise.

Davidson had two security details waiting outside her front door in a black Audi A8 L Security (which offers VR10-level ballistic protection). Such a cool car. It offers a limited supply of fresh air, should the situation command it. I made a mental note that we needed to explore these after this mission was over. Its armor protected against 7.62mm, as well, and it could withstand two DM51 hand grenades. Sweet ride.

It was time for Bethany to work. As we exited the van, we went to the back of it to grab cleaning supplies. Bethany grabbed a mop, causally looked back to Jake and me, and stated, "Watch how it's done. Be ready." Dressed in black trousers and a white revealing top, she started walking to the neighbor's house.

Picture Halle Berry in *Die Another Day*. Bethany was a looker and knew how to use it. As she walked beside the Audi, she casually tripped on the sidewalk and did a full-front sprawl onto the Davidsons' lawn and grabbed her ankle in anguish. Both security detail members jumped out to assist our poor gorgeous lady in distress. Big mistake. Huge.

Just goes to show you that even the best training can go out the window if you think you can score a piece of ass. The driver went to grab Bethany's arm to assist her back up, while the second detail went to grab the mop that she'd purposely thrown five feet away.

Jake and I shot them at the same time with our tranquilizing darts, and they were lights out, doing faceplants right beside our impromptu victim.

"Nice belly flop," I offered.

"Hope you can fly your ass home. Next time, you can do it. It's not as easy as you think. Personally, I'd give me a 9, on that one."

"Shoot me now," Jake protested. "Hurry up and let's get them in the van."

We lugged the two dupes into the van and Jake and Bethany donned black suit jackets over their attire, with some black Oakley Whisker sunglasses. Grabbing the earpieces, we waited for Davidson to instruct us that she was ready to exit her residence. Not even two minutes later, we got the request. Jake walked to the door to retrieve Davidson. She paid no attention to the man retrieving her at the door as she made haste to the vehicle. Jake opened the door for her, where she promptly plopped her butt in the seat only to be greeted by her spitting image looking right back at her, and my Gen

4 Glock Combat Carry pointed at her forehead. I wish I could have captured the moment on camera. Priceless. She may have sharted, as there was a distinct smell. I only hoped she didn't permanently mess up this fine vehicle.

"I had hoped I would have a little more time. I have something for you," she stated nervously in broken sentences as she attempted to reach into her satchel. I grabbed her hand forcefully before she could reach inside and indicated that was not a wise decision.

"Right now, we have other plans." With that, I jabbed her in the neck so she could join her detail in a long slumber.

TWENTY-SIX

WHILE WE WERE IN DC, Bes and Lily were working their magic overseas. While our day started at 9:00AM EST, Bes was nine hours ahead, and Lily fourteen hours into the next day. I called Tom and Steve, who were coordinating their efforts on our way to the Pentagon, and asked for the update on them.

Tom elected to go first and had me put him on speaker. "Well, we're all good, over in Russia. Bes was able to capture Heinrich and has him at the secure facility."

"Good. Just in time. Do we know how he managed to accomplish this? Any injuries? Fatalities? Or other necessary, pertinent information?"

"According to Bes, it was clean and simple. He had his wife, Alex, seduce him at a really nice Italian restaurant for lunch and she persuaded him to go back to The Ritz with her. From there, it was bag, tag, and transfer."

"What was the Italian restaurant? Can't imagine there are too many good ones, there."

"I don't remember what he told me. Something like LaScala or something."

"Hmm. We'll have to try it out the next time we are in town. How's Heinrich adjusting to his new accommodations?"

"Heard he pissed himself a few times."

"About what I expected. No good criminals ever think about the repercussions, do they? We feel confident that there will be no blowback?"

"Each of the board members has been sent dossiers that should ensure their silence. Bes has two men on each of them. He said something like he'd be staying at The Ritz a little longer with his surveillance team."

"I'm sure he will, since he's expensing it to me, the fucker. Probably with that little rat dog he has, too. So, Steve, what do we know from Lily's camp? Start with Li."

I could hear Steve clear his throat and stall a second. "Well, let's just say, it didn't go as smoothly as Bessum, but Li is in custody."
Ah, shit.

"Spill it."

"Well, do you want to hear her side first, or the digging around that I did?"

"I'm about three minutes out, so how about the abbreviated version now, and later you can fill us in on the details."

"I'm not sure you want to know the details later, either, but anyways… Hmm. Long story short…She has custody of Li. I'm not sure he has any...um, how do I say this…I don't think he has any bodily fluids left. Suffice it to say he had a smile on his face, but that may have been due to the loss of oxygen. Can't confirm."

"Holy shit. I don't want to know any more right now. Just answer me this: will he be able to resume normal mental capabilities in next 1-2 hours? He does us no good, if not."

"It may take a hot sec, but he should be able to regain full composure. We may have to medically ramp him back up."

"Please tell me you mean mentally, not sexually. I wouldn't put it past her to have his severed dong in her hand. And, where are we on Cheng Long?"

"The Chief of Chinese Media, owned by the CCP, is in custody, too. In fact, coincidentally, he was obtained the same time as Li, AND in the same condition..." *God help us.*

TWENTY-SEVEN

Washington, D.C.

THE PENTAGON HAS PARKING PERMITS for authorized personnel, and they strictly enforce mandates to obtain the names of all individuals and vehicles when parked on the Reservation. Each major component (Army, Air Force, Navy/Marines, and Chairman of the Joint Chiefs of Staff) has a designated representative who manages the allocation of parking. We were already cleared when we overtook the Audi. We had a third-party asset meet us to transfer Davidson and the security team, shortly after we detained them. Davidson wouldn't be returning to her home ever, with the security team only to be released after we concluded our business.

Upon arrival, we were greeted by a Lieutenant Protzman and were escorted to the Command Center. Unlike the movie *War Games* with Matthew Broderick, the actual Command Center (NMCC) includes several war rooms across twenty-one thousand square feet, can house over three hundred personnel, and isn't funded by the Joint Staff, but by the Department of the Air Force. Go figure.

Upon entering NMCC, Jake and Bethany would no longer be able to escort me inside. Here's where it was going to get complex. I would have to find a way to be alone with Adams, entering under the disguise of Davidson with no ability to predict who or what I would run into, with limited or no assistance.

Tom and Steve were monitoring all incoming personnel and visitors, but there're thirty thousand employees on a given day, not including visitors. We were tapping into the actual facial recognition programs that the Pentagon uses, thanks to some assistance from the "real" President. I had a hard stop of forty-five minutes from entering to procure what I needed before the shit hit the fan.

I walked in and started making the rounds with small talk before Adams eyed me and gave a subtle nod and smile, acknowledging my presence. Her demeanor appeared to relax when she saw me. She was probably relieved due to the fact that Davidson was the one person who could place Adams in collusion with the other countries and agencies. *The enemy of my enemy is my friend.* At the present moment, Adams only had one friend. I was about to change that.

Twenty minutes passed. My timing needed to be exact. There were currently thirty people in the room. The Chief and Vice Chief of Staff for the Air Force were both present, along with several members of the President's senior advisors for Communication, Strategic Planning, and Policy. Damn, it was a who's who of DC. They had no idea what was about to transpire.

Thirty minutes and counting. I was in conversation with the Vice Chief and excused myself to make a call. Cell phones had new restrictions and were prohibited in the Pentagon except in common areas due to the sensitivity of classified information. I would be using a land line that would be traced to a burner.

"Everyone in place?"

"Got your 6."

"Get ready for FUBAR."

"Lima Charlie."

I stayed seated by myself and looked around the room for Adams. Upon making eye contact, I did a subtle nod to indicate for her to come over. I only hoped she would promptly abide without me having to disrupt her present conversation with her Chief of Staff. Thirty seconds, followed by another minute. *Time is a ticking.* I made a mental note of "patience is a virtue" and mentally recited Matthew 5:9 - *Blessed are the peacemakers for they shall be called sons of God.* Of course, in this age of political correctness, 'sons' has been changed to children. *Focus, dammit.*

Adams was peeling away and coming towards my direction. Thirty-five minutes down.

She approached the conference table and grabbed my hand with a firm squeeze as she seated herself beside me. *Oh, shit.* It wasn't a 'glad you are here' squeeze, it was a little more… intimate. *Oy.* That would explain a few more things.

She looked at me with her weary eyes and asked, in a hushed but urgent, tone, "Are all of our tracks covered?"

In a sense.

"Madam President. I'm afraid you have run into a situation."

A few common signs to identify fear in others include rapid heartbeat, shortness of breath, trembling, and sweating. That, or the dead giveaway when the person's eyes go as wide as a saucer. Adams had immediate perspiration forming on her frontal lobe, illuminating even more her eyes, that easily could have been mistaken as a Tarsiers primate. Creepy mofos.

Adams now vacillated from fear to anger as she assessed correctly that something was about to go down. Calmly, facing away from me, she stated, "I think you have a pronoun problem, Kelly. There is no you, but only us, going forward. If anything happens to me, you too will suffer the full consequences of the Office of the President."

There have been a few Presidents in the US history that have been charged with criminal misconduct. You had Andrew Johnson, who was impeached over post-Civil War policies but later acquitted. Ulysses S. Grant was arrested for speeding. VP Spiro Agnew was charged with tax evasion. Nixon was charged with obstruction of justice and abuse of power before he quickly resigned. The difference between now and then? Social media. No President could have withstood their scrutiny, had they been charged in current times. Adams would be the first.

I turned my body to the side and looked directly in her eyes. I grabbed her hands not in the same fashion that she had just done, but in a preventative measure, to ensure she would not overreact to the next sentence.

"Madame President, I'm afraid you are mistaken. I am certainly not Kelly. I'm sure she sends her regards from where she is being detained."

If Adam's eyes weren't saucers before, they were now. She attempted to pull back, but I held on firmly as she rapidly related, "One look, one word, from me is all it takes to have you arrested, or better yet, killed."

"Yes, you could, but that would expose you, more than me, now, wouldn't it? You play chess, Nancy? I'm afraid you are a few plays behind. This IS checkmate."

Neuroscientists computed that the human brain can process entire images in as little as thirteen milliseconds. Right now, she had just processed that she was FUBAR. We had the acting President with intent to (mass) murder, weapons threats, weapons of mass destruction, harboring terrorists, helping to finance terrorist activity, federal conspiracies on so many levels it's not worth time to list, cybercrimes, collusion…shit, at this point, we were just missing child pornography, but I wouldn't put it past her. Only two previous Presidents have been impeached, but neither were convicted. This wouldn't be the case for Adams, nor would it be her only option.

Forty-four minutes.

"Under your seat is a handgun with one bullet. It's your choice on how you use it."

"What's to stop me from using it on you?"

"Nancy, don't be dense, now. Again, it would implicate you more than me. We all have free will, for a reason. How's that sphincter muscle of yours? That's your other option." I winked.

"You're bluffing."

"I take offense. My parents taught me never to bluff if you couldn't afford to play. Look up at the monitors. I'll leave you with these little nuggets to aid in your decision."

I got up and started walking to the door to exit. My back was to her, and she could have, at any moment, chosen to shoot me or have me arrested. Her primal instincts knew that she had to know, first, what was about to transpire.

One by one, the monitors started to populate slowly with pictures. First, Li came on the screen. Then, Snape. Next, Long. No audio, only visuals. Pandemonium kicked in as the Pentagon's secure network was hacked. I turned before I reached the exit to see the sheer shock and disbelief on Adam's face. The next picture to populate was the deathblow. Our real Commander in Chief appeared on the screen. His audio wasn't muted, and he could be heard saying, "I AM alive. My name is Easton Borrelli, and I AM the President."

Machiavellianism is the ability to manipulate and use whatever means necessary to gain power. Adams was a psychopathic bitch. Her narcissism had elevated with her collusion with China. She wanted a legacy, while they got the economy.

She left a legacy, alright. All over the table, chair, and walls.

I wonder what went through her mind. I'd like to think that the last thing that went through her head, other than that bullet, was to wonder how the hell Matti Baker and her team ever got the best of her.

TWENTY-EIGHT

I WAITED OUT THE PENTAGON'S lockdown procedures as I transformed myself back to me. Records produced would show that I was among the authorized personnel on file, visiting for an official US Department of Defense meeting that was scheduled at the exact moment that Adams took her life.

I rejoined Bethany and Jake, and after two days, we departed to return to our new home base in Colorado.

Once back at our new compound with Freddy, Tom, and Steve, we all gathered to rehash the events that had transpired and speculate would happen over the next couple months. The term 'carpe diem' was created by a Roman poet, Horace, and means 'to seize the day', intended to express the idea that one should enjoy life while one can. We were going to put this into practice. 'Work hard, play hard', was our motto.

I couldn't afford to contact Borrelli. He'd asked for my assistance to "get it done." He gave no direction on how. He knew what he was asking, without asking it. Quite frankly, the less he knew, the better. It's a tricky walk over what is acceptable in the name of defending our country. Were we the same as our adversaries? No worse, no better? We must individually wrestle with that internal struggle.

I'd had no guarantees or prediction that Adams would take her own life. I'd just played the stock market, making an educated guess based off the information at hand. You must choose wisely.

TWENTY-NINE

OVER THE NEXT WEEKS, THE BIGGEST PIECE, obviously, was the return of the President and Vice President and the implications that had on multiple levels, organizations, agencies, and individuals. This wouldn't be like when Clinton was cited with obstruction of justice or perjury, or even Trump with inciting violence, but took it to a whole new level. Colluding with countries to manufacture and release a deadly virus on the public was a whole new ballgame. The President and Vice President being in hiding while they devised a workable solution was another extraordinary issue. These were unprecedented times.

Easton (I mean, Mr. President) would need to sort that out over the next months, most probably through a second term, and for generations to come. His legacy would be built on finding ways to protect Americans at all costs, while juggling the digital era and ramifications of the effort. My team couldn't perform miracles (*although, I'd argue, we were damn close on most days),* but this was his fight. Of course, we'd pledged a long time ago to serve at the pleasure of the President, and would continue, if he wanted us to. I believed in him. I just hoped he would live up to it.

A military journalist, David Hackworth, once said, "If you find yourself in a fair fight, you did not plan your mission properly." As a nation, we have failed miserably on many fronts.

The public, nationally and globally, and the developments with the demise of Adams and how all this could play out in the first place was another complete war, in itself. Once again, social media would be used to divert the real issues while Congress explored options for antitrust laws and companies while also paying out trillions for federal relief. Let's call it what it is: hush money. It's never good when you rely on the government, and the long-term implications would impact future generations to come.

Davidson was picked up at the Headquarters of Homeland Security in what appeared an inebriated state, where she strenuously objected that she was not at the Pentagon at the time of Adam's death. (Did she not watch *A Few Good Men*?!) Video surveillance and interactions with senior officers at the Pentagon proved otherwise. She was awaiting sentence, with no bail. The documentation that she had procured to profess her limited interactions was suddenly MIA. Unlike in the *Hunger Games*, the odds were not forever in her favor.

Roman Wagner miraculously was detained and charged with collusion and conspiracy. He, too, was awaiting trial with no bail, and was detained at the little jail in the basement of the Capitol. He never made it to the facility, as a Jeffery Epstein-style death awaited him. The Attorney General stated that it was culmination of errors by guards on duty that allowed him to take his own life. As a result of his death, the charges were dismissed. The US had bigger issues to tackle.

Li, Snape and Long were removed from their positions by their respective countries and quickly replaced with new predecessors. None of them were heard from again, and this generated speculation and new conspiracy theories, that they were all assassinated. Know what the difference is between murder and assassination? To the receiving victim, technically none, but murder is the killing of one person by another. Assassination is when an important person is killed for political or religious reasons.

China and Russia, of course, claimed foul play by individuals only, and attempted to state that they were not privy, as a country, in the wrongdoings. *Shame on me once, shame on you twice.* As a nation, the US was operating on Defcon 2 for the foreseeable future.

We finally had the long-overdue private funeral service for Doug. It was just our team in attendance. It weighs on me. After all these years in service, he was my first team loss. *Oh, Doug. I'm so sorry, my dear friend.*

Tom and I spent the next few weeks with the kids and dogs, while Steve and Bethany charted a yacht to sail the British Virgin Islands. Jake was with Freddy mending a broken heart, as Chanlor was in custody for her role in Doug's death.

Despite everything, I knew I was operating under willful ignorance, avoiding becoming informed and forced to make an undesirable decision based on a desire not to think about the outcome. *Hot damn.* I couldn't avoid it any longer. I had to address the elephant in the room. It wasn't Li, Snape, foreign countries, or internal agencies.

I was a product of our government's intention to manufacture a biological weapon of mass destruction (with assistance from other countries).

Freddy showed me the latest report I'd requested. I wonder if he knew about or had suspected the results the entire time. I silently cringed when I read it. The real reason Wagner kept Chanlor close to the breast, and why she was elevated throughout her career, was that she was an offspring of one of my biologically produced brothers...therefore, making her my niece and my children's cousin.

We were a manufactured virus, and it was mutating. The stark revelation was that I was never and no longer alone. I closed my eyes as Linkin Park's, *In the End,* reverberated loudly, drowning out all other thoughts... *I kept everything inside and even though I tried, it all fell apart. What it meant to me will, eventually, be a memory of a time when I tried so hard...*

THIRTY

Colorado

TOM AND I DROVE TO DENVER to meet up with the good Doc. In my head, I played the different scenarios and outcomes over and over. Tom tried to gently reassure me and reminded me not to fret until I knew more. What was the point, right? Tom's calm demeanor was exactly what I needed. Always. He was my balance.

Doc ran a battery of tests and scans on me with a full physical and blood work-up. He asked us to stay in town for the night while he meticulously went over all the results. We opted to stay the Halcyon in Cherry Creek and eat at our favorite Italian restaurant, Quality Italian. We shared a bottle of 2016 Gaja Alteni di Brassica on the outdoor patio and reminisced about how we'd met and what had transpired over the years. A chance encounter that really wasn't at the Chateau Marmont in California, which seemed like ages ago. I knew when I first saw him, he did, too.

"Matti, no matter what the doc says, you understand that you have given your life and years to protecting the American people. You don't owe any more to any person, country, or government. You have always done more than you were asked, even with me and the kids."

"Shit, sounds like you're crafting my resignation speech."

"Sorry. I didn't mean it to come off that way. I just think we need to talk about realistic expectations. It's not because you are 'older'. I just think you have done everything you need to do. It's time for others to step up and take the lead. Let Borrelli do his job."

"And the night was going so well…" I teased back to him.

"God, Family, and Country is what you always said to me. Let's enjoy our family and let the others take care of the country."

"Oh, babe, that's why I have to follow this through. Don't you understand? Me. These results. It affects our family. Maybe not today, maybe not tomorrow, but our children will be wanted. Targeted. At all costs. Just like I have been targeted all my life. We are special, but that's not a bad thing."

He knew all too well that Mama Bear was not going to let anything harm our children. Grizzly bears spend less than two years bringing up their cubs, and mama bears can be quite harsh in correcting them. The cubs grow up with a healthy respect for their mothers which lasts long after they leave. I wasn't a fucking bear, though; I would never leave them to defend themselves unless I was positive that they were ready. We weren't there yet.

"Should we order another bottle?" *Nice deflection by him.*

"Sure. Carpe diem."

We met Doc the next day, to go over the results. He started his conversation casually. More casually than normal. The hairs on the back of my neck were rising as I sensed impending danger based on what he was about to share.

There was a slight tear in my meniscus, as I had suspected. I was more surprised by his next statement. "Generally, at your age, we'd see the tear and recommend surgery. But, it's completely healed. In fact, other previous bone breaks you have had are also completely healed. In fact, you wouldn't be able to tell you'd broken them. Had I not set most of these breaks myself, I wouldn't believe it. It's as though you never had them."

A person of my age? WTF!

I wondered: if I was a male in this profession, would he have said that? I was still lamenting on that line when he delivered the real blow.

"As fascinating as that is, the bigger, concern, Matti…is that it appears you'd previously contracted the virus. I'm assuming you didn't know, based off your questionnaire, and were asymptomatic."

"We were tested repeatedly. Each time, negative results."

"I'm afraid you were a false negative, as you carry the antigens. In a normal person, that would be fine; but for you, it appears to be mutating into something entirely new. I'm going to need to consult with outside experts, as this is out of my league, at this point. We need a particular specialist. We're going to need to test and compare your original vials, if we want to predict the outcome successfully and explore options to address, if needed…"

This had ramifications for ol' Doc, too. The last doctors that performed tests/surgery on me were paid never to work again. I'm sure he realized this when he told me this information, as it put his life in jeopardy, as well.

I thought about the vials twenty-four, seven. In the cold tundra of the Artic Circle, Bethany and I had deposited them in the Svalbard Global Seed Vault for preservation to ensure that no entity or country would possess them. I was going to have to return, to get them. Bethany was going to be pissed, as she hates the cold.

Although I've always considered myself different from others, I'm also similar, in many respects. A doctor tells you foreboding

news, and your first reaction is to craft your own obituary. *Holy shit.*
So messed up.

"What are you not telling me?"

"It's your blood. I've never seen anything like it before. Your genetic makeup and this variant of a virus are playing war inside your body. I'm surprised you have not had more severe symptoms. From a medical point of view, it's fascinating."

Gee, great. Think. Think. Think. Tell me a patient that reveals all their true symptoms to their doctor. In general, we are too embarrassed, self-absorbed, and guilty, to share all the intimate details. It's like when they ask how many drinks you consume a week, and you say five. I had four drinks last night, so what is the probability I have only one more before the end of the week? *Zero.* All patients tell terra diddles to their doctors, for self-preservation. The irony.

I had noticed other changes that I didn't divulge to the good doc. Maybe because Tom was in the room, and I didn't want to confess I'd noticed an increase in the amount of my body hair. Like, a freakish amount. Thank God for lasering. Or, I had a harder time with focus. Or, the fact I couldn't remember my kids' middles names for a few hours. I can disassemble and put back together a FN FAL semi-automatic in five seconds flat with no problem, though. *Fuuuuuck, what if I'm not special, after all?*

Vanity = stupidity.

"What are you really not saying?"

"From what I am witnessing, your genes will continue to mutate, and eventually one will win out over the other, or become something new. What it will become is the mystery we need to sort out. If you contracted this virus, we should assume that your children will be affected. We'll need to bring them in to test, also.

Their path may be different that yours—possibly even escalated, due to their age and hormones. We have no knowledge or expertise in this field to predict what will emerge."

With those words sinking in, I realized that my family was no different than the show *The Boys*. Myself, my unknown brothers, my children, and a niece possessed engineered abilities prone to do horrendous things, in secret. Not all of us were on a quest to do good. What would we transform into? How many more of us were there?!

The stark revelation again hit me smack in the face. I had never been alone in this fight. That scared me the most.

THIRTY-ONE

Rome/Svalbard

BETHANY WAS LESS THAN THRILLED when I told her to cut her vacation short to take us on a jaunt across the world. She was a little more sympathetic towards me after I informed her of the doc's assessment. Mind you, just a little…she has a missing chip. Probably explains why we are best friends.

We were going to need to make a pit stop in Rome before we headed to Svalbard, which was halfway between Norway and the North Pole.

Between all my worldly travels, Rome was still one of my favorite location destinations. The atmosphere, food, and wine—it all culminates in a perfect setting. Definitely, you should go see the Colosseum, Trevi Fountain, St. Peter's Basilica, and the Square, but I could spend days in the Vatican and the Sistine Chapel. In order not to repeat history, you must learn history. With cancel culture on full-time gamut, we were self-inflicting certain doom.

The last time I traveled to Italy, I was on a mission to locate the Director of NSA, Paul Rodgers. I allowed Rodgers to escape my first encounter with him, but he met his ultimate demise when he was forced to parachute out of a purposefully stalled cargo airplane and his chute was 'damaged' thanks to my TAC-50 sniper rifle. Let's just say that he became one with the mountain.

Guess who oversees the protection of communication networks? Yeah, that falls under the NSA. I spend as much of my time on discovering, covering, and dismantling internal governmental agency conspiracies as thwarting outside countries' efforts. That's so messed up. Counterintelligence.

Due to the events of the US President(s) and global pandemic, a G20 summit was called, to convene in Rome. This meeting was comprised of twenty of the top countries to address major issues to achieve global economic stability and growth. Looks like they had a lot to catch up. The group assembles at least once a year with the head of government (or highest-ranking official) attending. Countries attending include: Argentina, Australia, Brazil, Canada, China, France, Germany, India, Indonesia, Italy, Japan, Republic of Korea, Mexico, Russia, Saudi Arabia, South Africa, Turkey, the United Kingdom, the United States, and the European Union.

Of course, there is the G7. It consists of Canada, France, Germany, Italy, Japan, the United Kingdom, the United States, and the European Union. Notice the absentee country: China.

With a global pandemic, vaccination conspiracies, government corruption and cover-up at the highest levels within multiple countries, the complete failure of timely removal of US troops in Afghanistan, and discord amongst races, religions and freedoms, these elected officials needed to convene for months. Two days was not going to cut it.

The US spends over four trillion, annually, on foreign aid, with Afghanistan receiving the most, as part of Operation Enduring Freedom. *Might want to consider renaming it something else.*

Strangely enough, without benefit or the knowledge of history, one wouldn't necessarily realize that all countries have started out under a dictatorship: a government in which one person or small group has unconditional power without effective constitutional limitations. We were fighting a war against terrorism and attempting to install democracy, and in turn, becoming the same thing we were fighting against.

There are five civil liberties in the US:
freedom of speech
freedom of press
freedom to assemble
religious freedom
freedom to petition the government

Four of these liberties are presently being infringed upon, so America, "Land of the Free" was on verge of being America, "Think like us or GTFO."

Each of the participating countries had a similar situation, which occurs when big business becomes too big. Amazon, ATT, Sinopec, ICBC, Gazprom…the list of the mighty that doesn't care about the few. Add in the likes of media conglomerates like News Corp, Sinclair, and the New York Times, and you have forces that were untouchable. *HEY, Houston, we have a problem!*

Palantir Technologies' CEO had a total compensation package of $1.098 billion. Yes, that's with a B. Hell, the Doordash CEO made almost half a billion. *WTF? I went into the wrong field of business.*

Rates for food, petrol, and everything else have risen by double and triple percentages, yet salaries and wages have barely risen, with Congress still fighting over legislation to increase the minimum wage from $7.25 an hour. That barely covers one Grande Carmel Macchiato from Starbucks. *Oh, that's another issue.*

So, twenty countries were coming together for two days to discuss how do we advert situation(s) in the future, and what remedies could be put in place to slow the spread of not just a deadly virus, but deal with vaccinations, climate change, inequality, and the civil unrest each of our countries faced independently.

I was asked to listen and observe only, and to report to the President if I felt that there was any backdoor activity happening that could potentially derail any efforts. Made me think of Al Pacino in the mini-series *Hunters...Monsters can be little. Monsters can be old. Hell, Monsters can be us...*

I changed my appearance to assume the identity of the Prime Minister of Australia, who was unexpectedly kept from traveling. Australia is (and has been) a vital ally to the US, and the Prime Minister willingly obliged with the prospect of helping the greater good.

The Prime Minister was also a "he", so my disguise skills needed to be on point for this op. Wrapping my chest was excruciating. Almost as bad as the fake prosthetic junk. Luckily for me, these meetings provided an opportunity to be concealed, with face masks still in place, and due to twenty foreign countries and twenty foreign languages ensuring interpreters and headsets on every individual. Bethany would be my assigned interpreter, and I had fun having her carry and hold my briefcase. She shot me the death look when I asked her to fetch a cup of coffee, and to be quick about it. I was confident I'd have to pay for that later.

Day one of the discussions, and my head was about to explode. Probably from the tightness of my chest wrapping, but it was like watching kindergarten children trying to figure out a sixth-grade puzzle. Sometimes, it just doesn't need to be this hard.

We adjourned for the evening's dinner and events in Rome. This is where I needed to focus. Although security precautions were put in place and on high alert, would you feel comfortable knowing that the world's leaders were all congregated in one location, which they have shared to the entire world? Remember *Clear and Present Danger* when they remote-bombed the shit out of all the cartel drug lords that had all gathered secretly?

Fiction was becoming factual. I had no desire to be in the same place as twenty other known assassins (I mean, delegates).

I've played dead before, and had no desire to repeat it in the near future. I had my own issues to address.

So, I skipped out of the evening festivities and joined Bethany back at the suite. We had set up surveillance and mic'ed up a few of our common culprits to follow them; namely China, Russia, India, and, for good measure, we added Mexico. It's advantageous to know the language of your enemy, and lucky for us, despite best attempts to feign ignorance, that our enemies all knew and spoke English fluently.

We sorted through the conversations. There were conversations and chuckles on the release of unclassified UFO sightings by our country's Director of National Intelligence. The pictures they released to the public were so blurry, it was a joke. We've had the technology and capability to see, from satellites, the whites of your eyes since the early 1960s. Why even bother releasing these? *Rhetorical: they had to, under the Release of Information Act.* Anything they were trying to obscure had already been privy to other countries, and apparently the public was ok with what they distributed. Confirmation bias at its finest.

Heated discussions occurred between China and India over

global climate changes. More specifically, the impact of the distribution of water. With each country having over one point four billion people, China and India both get their water source from the Himalayans, and the region is not producing enough to allocate for both countries, collectively.

With population peaks projected for the year 2030, water shortage would be an ongoing problem, and new wars would be started.

In fairness, living now in Colorado, the Colorado River was in short supply, supplying lower amounts to seven states. Companies are buying individuals' water wells under eminent domain and then telling them to purchase bottled water. Government at its finest. BTW, Ozarka is owned by Nestle and Coca-Cola, in a joint venture of Beverage Partners Worldwide. Its slogan is that they have "naturally spring water" that goes through a ten-step purification process. Ten steps. *Hmmm.*

My mission was to identify and stop activities designed to prevent or thwart spying, intelligence gathering, and sabotage by an enemy or other foreign entity. Of course, I was also spying on our own selves. Counterintelligence.

As we scrutinized each conversation over the two-day retreat and observed the interactions of each country, Bethany and I continued to notice one thing, consistently: Mexico was awfully quiet. Too quiet.

THIRTY-TWO

IT WOULD BE JUST BETHANY AND I, as we loaded and boarded the G650ER to take off to the Global Seed Vault to procure the vials. I must admit, these were my favorite times. Just two gals, hamming it up. There's a certain creature comfort of having your best friend since sixteen. We needed to share just a look to complete a sentence or a thought. Between training, missions, marriage, childbirth, relationships, we'd shared in it together.

I technically owned fifty-two percent of 'our' company and had ultimate say in decisions, but also handled the majority of the risks and operational costs. She was fine with that. Bethany freelanced on the side, as well, if time permitted, but her loyalty came first to our ventures and, thankfully, to my family. When I was being rebuilt, she stepped in to take care of my family. I'd kill for her. Like me, too, she was fiercely protective of our nation and country.

The seed vault is a long-term depository that has deposits from across the globe. It now has over one million varietals for essential food crops and plant species, and can accommodate up to four million selections. It was established in 2008 to help in event of mismanagement, natural disasters, equipment failure, etc., but it has largely been speculated that its true intent was to help rebuild in the event of a large-scale or global catastrophe. We should all pray that we would utilize these services later versus sooner.

The Norwegian government funds the upkeep with support from some hefty donors, like those billionaires that go by their last names.

On autopilot over the Norwegian Sea, we opted for a game of chess to pass the time. Normally, we'd have a bottle of something delicious to accommodate us while we discussed world problems, but it was only us on this trip, so we had to keep our wits about us.

"Do you think the visit to Rome was a colossal waste of time?" she asked as she started the game and moved her pawn to F3. *She's going to regret that move.*

"No. Other than not being able to go to some of our favorite spots, I think we observed and have noted interactions between countries that we need to follow up on."

"What have you told the kids about your diagnosis and the probable impact on them?

Dammit. I just didn't want to have to address this, yet. "We haven't told them anything, yet. We didn't want them to worry until we had more concrete information. We will after we bring back the vials for Doc to run tests and compare." I casually moved my pawn to E5.

"Does Doc McHottie realize that he probably won't be working in the public sector anymore, after this?"

"He's a smart man. I'm sure he calculated, at some point in this doctor-patient relationship, that this was a high probability. The financial impact will lessen some of his concerns, and he'll still be able to perform his trade for discreet patients."

Bethany moved her pawn to G4. *Bahaha.*

"What about the seven scientists that we captured last year? What is their status? I mean, we have China, Russia, Afghanistan and, worst of all, 'us', conspiring to coding modifications at the highest levels. I'm not sure how the US will recoup, after this year.

"I mean, really, they were attempting to duplicate these vials that created you. We are already in a global pandemic, with mutating variations that could lead to global genocide, if distributed in a worldwide solution (which appears to be the case, as no one is listening to reason anymore)."

I moved my Queen to H4 and announced, "Checkmate."

"God dammit, in two moves. How did you do that?" she asked incredulously.

"A little luck, but I've learned it's helpful to think two steps ahead. Another game?"

"Screw you." she scorned.

"Didn't take you for a sore loser."

"Can you fly the plane home? How's that for two moves ahead?" she offered.

"Haters gonna hate. Cards, then, Princess?"

"I really dislike you, some days," she grumbled as she grabbed the stack of cards.

"I love you, too."

THIRTY-THREE

Colorado

OBTAINING THE VIALS WAS UNEVENTFUL, and we returned to the Colorado compound to meet up with the team. Where I would (re)deposited them would be another matter that had me more apprehensive, as the hunt for them would only escalate even further.

For the remainder of the trip home, I deliberated the status of the seven scientists that Bethany had brought up. We had seven scientists that had previously been in Antarctica and who were suspected of trying to recreate and distribute a deadly virus—potentially, the same virus that had been used in my creation.

We'd captured the scientists in Kandahar, relocated them to Area 51, and had had them under Ainsworth's surveillance until the pandemic broke out. *Did they help cause it? Or were they working on a bigger scenario?* When the outbreak of the virus hit, we relocated Ainsworth to help Jake and Steve with the training program in Colorado, and had Retired Sergeant Larkin take over the watch on the scientists. Larkin, despite being American, had a thick Irish accent, and was a big conspiracy aficionado about Mars and space travel. He swore that we had a contingency force that was secretly sent to space, and that was why the Space Force branch was created. He was the perfect choice to take over surveillance at Area 51.

Although it was known that Freddy and I were no longer 'dead', strangely enough, we weren't necessarily on anyone's radar. People really are stupid. Misdirection and gaslighting were mainstays in this current environment and the new go-to PC verbiage. We used to simply term it 'someone being a dick.' Now we used the term 'gaslighting' when an abuser controls a victim by twisting their sense of reality.

We'd studied these techniques extensively in training. After all, people in my profession tend to be on a certain spectrum of our own. I've been on heightened alert for decades, so why now, after everything that has gone down, had our enemies stood down in trying to locate us? I wasn't buying it.

I asked everyone to meet up in the great room in ninety minutes so I could take off for a quick run to help clear out the last few days of travel. I always did my best thinking when on the move. I hoped that today would be no exception.

I popped in my earbuds and shuffled while I searched for my other favorite Tom. *No, not Tom Brady*. The one and only original, Tom Petty. *May he rest in peace*. I started on a fast pace despite listening to *Square One…Square one, my slate is clear, rest your head on me, my dear. It took a world of trouble, took a world of tears, it took a long time to get back here…*

Every individual has a predisposition mindset that will subconsciously direct you to what you are needing or wanting. It's why you watch a certain movie over and over, or read your favorite book again. You need or want that feeling that it elicits. Same way your body has a craving for a certain food. It's telling you what you need to do to refuel.

My brain was trying to tell me something. I just needed to flesh it out. The elevation of the trails around the compound were steep, but I was having no trouble keeping and exceeding my normal pace. I couldn't remember the last time I'd beat my pace. Twenty-five minutes into the run, I wasn't slowing down. In fact, I was speeding up. Shit, I could have won in the Olympics, at this pace. I could feel, in my quads, the blood pumping through my veins and going to my heart. Pure adrenaline. *Oh, God, got to get that song out of my head.* I shuffled through some more songs, skipping over Lorde, Bieber, and few others before landing on *Nirvana, Smells Like Teen Spirit.* I mean, how could you pass up that song, right? By now, my pace was almost frantic. *WTF was going on?* I hadn't hit this level in roughly twenty years. Dammit, I WAS mutating. Just like Doc had theorized.

I had already turned around at my designated half point mark and was literally flying on the trail, on the return. Tom Petty shuffled back on with *I Should Have Known It.* My brain was telling me what I was needing to hear, but wasn't allowing…*I should have known it, hard to believe, it was all right there, in front of me…*

How did I miss it, before? We were going to need to bust out Chanlor.

THIRTY-FOUR

I CAME BACK FIFTEEN MINUTES ahead of schedule. I was a stickler for schedules. Arriving on time was being late. Period. Tom was in our bedroom getting changed when I came in and he inquired how my run was...*pretty fucking awesome*...but I responded with a simple "pretty quick, but I did come up with some new thoughts..."

"You always do. That's what I love about you. I'll see you downstairs. Anything you need me to do while you take a quick rinse? Want me to join you?"

"Next time," I smiled. "But, it would help me if you could look up something while I get cleaned up. Can you pull up that information on Wilson's mother and drill down deeper? I want to know her full backstory."

"On her mother? The one in the nursing home?"

"That would be the one."

"Hot damn. Why do I feel like we're about to go road tripping again real soon?"

"Well, a rolling stone gathers no moss."

"Oh, Lord."

I think Jake was getting used to the good life. I was going to have to give him grief. He had a plethora of appetizers and drinks organized on the buffet. Not that I was complaining, as I was famished. His wine selection was improving, as well, with Au Sommet decanted on the table.

After everyone ate, we seated at the round table. This table was huge, like in *First Knight* with Richard Gere and Sean Connery. Tom had selected this monstrosity since it represented that everyone was equal and trustworthy. We had to tear down a wall and use a crane to bring this table in, as it was too large to come through conventional means (aka a door). *By 'we', I mean Tom had to arrange it. Thank God he had a deep fondness for shopping.* Of course, we had to tear the same wall down again when he located the perfect chandelier to go over it. *I know, I know. First World problems.*

Once everyone was seated, we recapped events and gave an update on current timelines. I was making mental notes when I blurted out, "I need to apologize, everyone. I think my pride interfered with this latest operation."

"Holy shit. Did she just apologize for something? Did anyone voice record that?" Steve blurted.

Light awkward chuckles throughout the room. Tom's eyes expressed surprise, mixed with concern. Freddy sat there motionless, understanding where this was going.

I disregarded num-nuts comment and proceeded. "Biblically, pride is the deadliest sin of all, the root of all evil and the beginning of sin. This whole time, I have been focused on me being the root cause, when, in reality, I should have been focusing more on others – which led me to miss some important leads."

"What are you talking about? It's a team effort. If something was missed, then we all missed it. You're not Wonder Woman," posed Bethany.

I turned towards Tom, who was sitting right beside me. "Tom were you able to find out more about Chanlor's mother?"

Jake perked up immediately. "What does Chanlor's mother have to do with anything?"

Freddy and I had not yet discussed with the group what we had learned about Chanlor being biologically related. Time to rip off the Band-Aid.

Tom started reading off his laptop. "Chanlor's mother was admitted into the DC nursing home almost two years ago, under psychiatric care for acute mental breakdown and unable to perform simple physical tasks by herself."

"I'm confused. What does this have to do with anything?" Jake questioned again.

"Hold on, we're about to get to that. Tom, how old was Chanlor's mother when she was admitted?"

Confusion and doubt were on everyone's faces as they looked to each other for some snippet of information to tie it all together.

"Let's see. Per her records, she would be…umm, wait, this doesn't sound right. She'd only be forty-two, right now. That doesn't make sense. Why would she be in a nursing home at that young age?"

"Let me rehash history first and then, Freddy, you can fill in any holes I may be missing…. Freddy and I drilled down to find out why Wagner, head of the FDA, was so tight with Chanlor's family. Long story short, Chanlor is an offspring of one of my two brothers. The experiment was supposed to conclude with twin boys, but I was born. A female. An unexpected anomaly. We were separated immediately at birth. My (well, 'our') mother detonated sarin nerve gas, killing everyone in the room, including herself and the doctors and scientists. Freddy had taken me, and my brothers were distributed to Russia and, at the time, the CIA. Like me, my siblings were being trained to be human weapons. I was to be the host for new generations, but with Freddy hiding me, the other countries used my brothers to procreate, in my absence. It appears they started them young. It's our belief that Wagner was instrumental in the birth of Chanlor. She shares in my biological makeup and therefore is my niece and my children's cousin, as a result of a brother I have never met."

"Holy shit. Get the popcorn out," interjected Steve.

Blink. Blink. Exhale.

"Anyways…two years ago, Chanlor's firm was contracted to fast track a vaccine. Two years ago...that would be one year before this virus hit. Her mother coincidentally goes into a nursing home at the ripe age of forty. Her injuries at the time of admission suggest she was beaten within an inch of her life. I believe they wanted the location whereabouts of 'Dad', aka one of my brothers. The mother hasn't talked since, nor will she ever. I'm sure that, after her death, they will find she had severe CTE, at admission."

Silence, as everyone processed what this meant.

"With Wagner's demise and Chanlor's mother not an option, we need to get access to Chanlor and see what she knows about her father or uncle, and their whereabouts. We also need her out, as she most likely is mutating, due to this virus, and we will need to ensure her and the public's safety.

Jake, who had an invested interest in her safety, asked, "So, are you now thinking she possibly was just an innocent bystander?"

I looked to Freddy for confirmation. "We don't have enough information at this time to confirm that conclusion."

"Why do you think she could possibly be mutating?" asked Bethany.

I looked to Tom with despair, then looked around, I placed my hands under the heavy oak and steel table and lifted it up easily on one side. "Because I am."

All mouths were wide open when they saw how easily I lifted the dead weight of this ginormous table. When confronted with something that's not easily explained, one has a tendency to flee, freeze, or fight. Luckily for me, everyone in the room was a trained professional; otherwise, it might have been pandemonium.

Steve, once again, broke the ice with, "Well, Tom, there's no shame in a woman who can kick your ass." *Damn, he could be funny.*

A little levity was needed, and that was exactly what transpired. As I glanced around, I humbly nodded, acknowledging the unspoken. "Tom and I are going leave immediately to get the kids. We'll need to have them examined, as well." With that, the closeness and the potential severity of the situation resonated throughout everyone.

Jake quickly offered, "What do you want us to do?"

"Take Steve and go get your girl and bring her back ASAP. Freddy and Bethany, start working some magic. We need to locate my brothers and figure out how many other 'children' may be out there."

THIRTY-FIVE

THE KIDS WERE LESS THAN NINETY MINUTES away from the compound, with thirty minutes of that just getting out of our own property. We called ahead and told them they'd be getting an unexpected training leave of seventy-two hours. They were thrilled.

Tom pulled up in the H2. I loved this car, which had us sitting up higher than everyone else. Great for off-roading, too, but the 2009 model was built for comfort and luxury, since it was the last year GM produced it. Of course, this vehicle had a few additional and necessary modifications added to it.

Tom held my hand as we drove, staring aimlessly at the road, before he asked, "How did you suspect the mother was younger?"

Fair question. "Remember that intel that Davidson was hoping to use in her defense? It included dossiers on Chanlor and Wagner. That quickly led me to arbitrate with Freddy. 'Freddy, you have some 'splaining to do,'" I said in my best Lucille Ball accent.

"Not funny, Matti. This is serious. What is Freddy's involvement, at this point?"

"To the best of my knowledge, he's juggling being a step-father and world domination. Not handling it great, but could be worse. I missed it originally, too. I saw that Chanlor's age was noted as twenty-seven, but wasn't computing that her mother would be only fifteen years older than her. As a society, we tend to assume that someone is old if they are in a nursing home. You know what happens when you assume?"

"But you knew when you asked me to pull it, didn't you?"

"I suspected it based on something entirely different. While I was off running today, I kept thinking back to the G20 summit. Every nation was in an uproar but one. Mexico. Why? Accusations were being thrown left and right, and they said nothing."

"When someone accuses you of something, if you don't say anything, then there's a high probability there is something to the accusation. Just saying. More importantly, the dossiers had information that Chanlor legally changed her last name when she turned twenty-one. Chanlor Wilson used to be Chanlor Sanchez."

"I'm not sure I'm following. How does Mexico fit in?"

"Mexico's heritage is infamously known for always valuing one's family as the most important aspect of life. It may be stereotyping or profiling, but Mexicans are known to be fiercely loyal to family, putting the interests of family above their own. I suspect the CIA initially made a secret deal for one of my brothers to have him hidden there for anonymity, or more likely so they could have plausible deniability. They'd claim they weren't privy or part of the initial experiment. Wagner's travel logs confirmed he made frequent trips to Mexico. Best guess? He was protecting an investment."

"Chanlor was brought here to the US right after she changed her name and began working at her firm and quickly moving up the ranks. She was being groomed and used by Wagner. When things started escalating with the virus (mind you, long before it was publicly announced), it's my conviction that more 'parties' started looking for the original hosts in hopes to conceal them permanently, manufacture more, or to use them for an antidote.

"Remember *Outbreak*? Borrelli had good intentions. Adams did not."

"They thought you were dead, so they started going after the brothers?"

"Exactly. Now, while China, the US, and Russia fought over the virus and the economy, Mexico had been silently waiting. With the export of marijuana, cocaine, and even avocados, their sales were projected to grow by over forty percent. The halting of distribution due to the virus was crippling their economy, as well.

"A good portion of these sales will be from US, with the increased legalization of marijuana throughout the States. Sometimes your frenemies are enemies, too.

"Now, what would you do if you were a highly trained operative with high-level access and your wife was beaten essentially to death, and your daughter was in a US jail being used?

"IF one of my brothers was brought up in Mexico, he'd certainly be machismo, so to speak. He'd be very proud and protective of his wife and daughter. He'd want revenge. At all costs."

"So, that's the reason you are having Jake bring her back? You're using her as bait?"

"When you say it that way, it doesn't sound so good. I'm flushing him out in the open in hopes that we can start a conversation. The three of us are the Alphas, so to speak. I'm hoping to bring this to Omega. I need to locate all the parties involved, for everyone's protection. We need to amplify our counterintelligence efforts if we want to protect ourselves."

"Does Borrelli know what you are attempting?"

"For our protection, at the present time, I think it's best not to reveal all our intentions until we have further confirmations. I trust

Borrelli, but for now, our motto is "hope for the best, plan for the worst."

"Shit, Matti. I have a feeling we're about to have a real life *Narcos* or *Queen of the South* scenario going on."

"Hmm. I was thinking more Mayan, but those work, too."

"You really need help."

THIRTY-SIX

I REMEMBER WHEN THE KIDS told me they wanted to follow in my profession, and we dropped them off for their first day of training. You can be a boohoo mom or a woohoo mom. I learned that day that I was a boohoo mom.

Not that I wasn't proud of them, but every parent worries about if they did all they could do to prepare their kids. Luckily for us, we had family - Jake, Steve, and Ainsworth - preparing them for any areas that we'd failed to cover.

There is nothing better than a long-awaited hug, and the kids wasted no time when we drove up and got out. I still see them as little kids, not the mature adults they were becoming. I wondered if I'd ever see them differently. They would always be my babies.

"Thank GOD you got us out of there," was the first thing Mark said as he jumped into the Hummer.

"Missed you too, love," I added.

"Why didn't you bring the pooches?" Mary sadly inquired.

"We wouldn't be able to fit everyone in."

"You could have driven Freddy's Suburban," added Matthew.

"Killing me. 'Great to see you, Mom and Dad.' You'll see the dogs soon enough," I laughed.

"So, what's the real reason we are out? Ainsworth gave us some BS about mandatory leave days. Like he'd ever follow protocols."

Tom looked towards me to see how I was going to approach it I went with complete transparency. I filled the kids in on what had been happening and why we needed to do further testing on all of us, for everyone's protection. Their resiliency always surpassed my expectations. Was it due to being brought up in this generation, or the lack of experience?

While artificial intelligence had certainly allowed this generation to read and see more than we were able to growing up, there is a distinct difference from experiencing it in real life. *Damn acronyms, I cringed when I read them from others - IRL, OMG, LMAO…My initial thought was always STFU.*

"We'll make a pit stop to see Dr. Rihani on the way back, and then will head to the compound to meet up with everyone. Dad bought some new ATVs to try out, for a little off-roading fun."

"Will Grandma and Grampy be there?"

"No. We haven't found the time to have them come to the new place, but we will soon. We can give them a call now since we have everyone together. They'd love to hear from us. I'm sure you are reaching out on your own while you are at training, right?"

By their lack of quick response, I think they received my subtle reminder. We called my parents and the kids updated them on their training, reminding them that they couldn't share a lot of details due to their security clearance. We talked about upcoming holidays and said that we were working on a schedule to get everyone together real soon.

Tom smiled at me when we hung up the phone. "What are you grinning about?" I inquired incredulously.

"You always amaze me, woman. You can defend our country and still plan the turkey feast for a family holiday. You truly are one of a kind."

"Well, technically, I'm a triplet, but I appreciate your point. Thanks, love. By the way, you just missed our exit."

It took over three hours to complete everything that Rihani wanted to test. He had hoped that I would have brought the initial vials for comparison's sake. After reconsidering, I told him (for his well-being, for now) that he'd have to use my past results and the genetic makeup of our blood markers. Too many people were looking for these, and I had risked life and death to conceal them, for decades.

I couldn't let go of control now. Not yet. We still had too many unanswered questions with the scientists, the virus, mutations, vaccinations, and the ultimate motives of individual countries and officials. Borrelli had effectively used social media to his advantage in concealing certain facts from the public. The irony was that this was his biggest policy agenda: to protect the American's liberties and freedom of rights. Do as I say, not as I do.

Once we obtained Doc's initial assessment, we would have our own laboratory we'd set up to further identify, locate, and replicate the virus, if necessary.

Of course, I was going to need to pinpoint a new permanent residence for the vials, as we couldn't risk having them on the property with us. I had them in my Dotting Grand Circle safe, a glorious masterpiece that had the likes of Las Vegas salivating, but you can't reason with crazy. With the virus suspected of being airborne, an attack on my property could have global ramifications. Don't forget: all aircraft and subs are nuclear powered, and any Tom, Dick, or Harry could get a drone from Amazon.

I was reminded of Proverbs 14:29: *A patient man has great understanding, but a quick-tempered man displays folly.* Patience was indeed a virtue. I wondered how long it would be before present society would try to rewrite that with 'person' versus 'man' Good lord, I should have taken Adams out when she ended her presidential address with "Amen and a woman." Trust me, I have patience. People truly can be stupid.

Once back to the main house, the kids went immediately to the dogs. Scout and Trooper were running in circles at the excitement, and even Koda and Bruiser let their guards down to join in on the merriment.

We jumped in the two new BMS-The Beast 1000 2S ATVs and took them off road on the property. We tested them on their claimed fourteen-foot ground clearance, and they passed with flying colors. These really were a fun escape, but they also involved some practical defensive maneuvering skills necessary for learning.

We took turns riding them all together, and then Tom and the kids split up and traded off riding. While they were off joyriding, I joined Freddy and Bethany on the back porch, and was caught up on potential sightings of the missing brothers. Jake and Steve successfully retrieved Chanlor with little fanfare (under the disguise of diplomatic immunity), to be returned after new questioning, and were on the way back.

Our new property really was majestic and serene. On the front side, we had views of large red rocks that resembled more of an Arizona landscape; and on the back side, we had the lush evergreen trees of the mountains. The howling winds over the mountain range in the morning hours provided a comforting atmosphere. The kids couldn't wait to see what the winter season would bring with snowfall on the property, with annual averages of one hundred inches.

The main residence had a wraparound patio for three-sixty views. The guest houses were scattered within the first mile of the main property, leaving acres on the back side to conceal an assortment of activity—namely our lab, ammunition warehouse, and an underground escape tunnel between facilities and residences.

Tom and the kids had returned from riding covered in dirt. The kids decided to take a quick shower first, before we all gathered for dinner. We had a lot to catch up on both individually and collectively. Jake and Steve had radioed in and said they would be at the front entrance in a few minutes. Tom decided to jump back in the ATV beast to meet them at the front of the property. He really enjoyed riding these and was like a little kid on them.

Freddy handed me a glass of The Judge Chardonnay and turned on the seventies channel on SiriusXM. The Bee Gees' *Stayin' Alive* quietly piped through the outdoor speakers…*Whether you're a brother or whether you're a mother, you're stayin' alive, stayin' alive. Feel the city breakin' and everybody shakin', and we're stayin' alive, stayin' alive…*

"How you are holding up, kiddo?"

"Good…just happy to have us all together in the same place."

"We have a lot of balls up in the air, right now. You ready for this next chapter?"

"As ready as we'll ever be, I suspect. I want to keep the convos a little light tonight, but tomorrow, we need to meet up in the situation room and hammer out some important details. I've asked Lily and Bes to sit in on a call. We're going to need their assistance in a few areas."

"Sounds good. How are you feeling? Any new discoveries? What did Rihani say?"

"You mean, can I bench press you right now, old man?" I said with a smile. "I feel great. In fact, never better. The question remains: will this be temporary or permanent? And...what we are all wondering...will it have any other long-term consequences for me (or, more importantly, for the kids)?"

"I can't tell you enough...every day, I wish I'd never let your mother go through with that experiment and I see what it's done to you, and now your family. All in the name of protecting America," he said, using his hands for air quotes. *People his age really should stay away from that. Well, anyone, really.*

"I know, Freddy. I truly do."

"I've made quite a few mistakes over the years when it's come to protecting your identity and our nation. I'm sorry, kiddo, that I choose poorly, at times."

"We all do the best that we can do with the information that we have on hand. Don't live in the past, Freddy. We just need learn from it."

We sat there in silence, overlooking the beautiful Colorado sunset. The dogs all joined us on the deck, with Scout and Trooper instantly asleep from playing for ten minutes with the kids. We really were going to need to put them on a diet, sooner than later. Koda and Bruiser appeared a little agitated. I assumed they were waiting for the boys to come back to the compound.

Bethany pulled a chair up to join us and poured a glass. "I could get used to these views. Not too shabby."

I sat with my head back on a recliner, soaking in the last rays of the day with the slight fall breeze and thinking that when this last mission was over, it was time to let the next generation take over. I was done. I had done everything my country asked, and even more. Each of us craves connection. I had committed myself to protecting America and my family, at all costs. It was time. I felt at peace, here.

Koda and Bruiser jumped off the deck and were going full speed to the front of the entrance. This was not normal. Dogs can hear twice as many frequencies as humans, and can hear over four times further away than humans. Bethany and I looked at each other before we recognized what we were hearing. Snipers can shoot silently as long as they are out over six hundred meters, as the bullet is traveling faster than the speed of sound. The cracking sound a bullet makes, though, can be heard by humans. We heard two.

Our eyes traveled to the location the dogs were heading, and instantly our hearts leapt as I screamed, "Tom!" while she mimicked with, "Steve!"

I screamed, "Freddy, get the kids into the bunker! Bethany, get to the recons!"

I jumped over the railing and was running at supernatural speed. They wanted a weapon, they got one.

While my heart said *Trust in HIM*, my mind went to Megadeth's *I'll Get Even* blaring through my conscious... *I'll get even with you, ah, that's what I'm gonna do (I'm gonna get even with you). I'll get even with you, even with you, even with you...*

The End is just the beginning.

COUNTERINTELLIGENCE
SPOTIFY
PLAYLIST

Bee Gees - Stayin' Alive
Bolt Thrower - No Guts, No Glory
Cure - Let's Go to Bed
Eagles - Lyin Eyes
Enimen - Lose Yourself
John Conlee - Rose Colored Glasses
John Waite - Missing You
Linkin Park - In the End
Marilyn Mason - We're Killing Strangers
Nick Lowe - God Help the Beast in Me
Nirvana - Smells like Teen Spirit
Peaches and Herbs - Reunited
Peter Gabriels - In Your Eyes
Phil Collins - I Don't Care Anymore
Republica - Ready to Go
Stabbing Westward - Save Yourself
Stefan Engblom - Pure Aderenaline
Talking Heads - Burning Down the House
They Might Be Giants - Dr Evil
Tom Petty - I should have Known It
Tom Petty - Square One

COUNTERINTELLIGENCE
MOVIES
& SHOWS

90 DAY FIANCÉ	JURASSIC PARK
A CHRISTMAS STORY	MAYANS
A FEW GOOD MEN	MILLENNIUM
AIR FORCE 1	MISSION IMPOSSIBLE
AMERICAN PRESIDENT	MURDER AT 1600
ARMAGEDDON	NARCOS
AUSTIN POWERS: THE SPY WHO SHAGGED ME	NINE TO FIVE
BAD BOYS	OUTBREAK
BATTLEBOTS	PRETTY WOMAN
BEVERLY HILLBILLIES	QUEEN OF SOUTH
BEVERLY HILLS COP	RAIN MAN
BOURNE IDENTITY	ROCKY IV
CAPTAIN SULLY	SILENCE OF THE LAMBS
CASINO ROYALE	SONS OF ANARCHY
CLEAR AND PRESENT DANGER	SOPRANOS
COBRA KAI	TAKEN
DAVE	TENET
DIE ANOTHER DAY	TERMINATOR 2
FACE OFF	THE BOYS
FIRST KNIGHT	THE GENTLEMEN
HOME ALONE	TOMBSTONE
HUNGER GAMES	TOP GUN
HUNTERS	WAR GAMES
INDEPENDENCE DAY	ZERO DARK THIRTY

NOTE FROM THE AUTHOR

The only universal truth there is amongst all races, religions,
sexuality: we are born, and we die.

Invest in people.
Try talking.
Listen.

My books are intentionally kept shorter to read on a long flight or
day of vacation.
Relax, Enjoy, Think, Recharge,
and then go out and LIVE LIFE.

Ok, now that I got that (common sense) out of the way.
How'd you like the book? Fun, right?!
Stay tuned.

P.S. How many authors give you great music, movie, and other
author recommendations?

Just saying.

ACKNOWLEDGMENTS

To my Instagram family that has helped me learn this crazy book industry from formatting, covers, writing styles, and promotion, who supports me in so many more ways that I can't count. Thank you. A *special* thanks goes to:

@trippainsworth – Best Sci-fi military series out there. If you enjoy humor, relationships, Martians, military, and laugh-out-loud moments, you need to read The Smokepit Fairytales series. He's an incredible writer, artist, musician, and champion for the human spirit. Hell, he's even a recurring character in my books. Tripp, I hope we get to do a SiriusXm show one day, we'd kill it! #coors #jamesson
https://www.smokepitfairytales.com

@tamstales32 - Paranormal romance series, that is hot! I don't even like romance stuff, but I do now. She also has a rock series you don't want to miss out on. She is my sister from another mother and is also a huge advocate for other writers. Tam, I'm meeting up with you, so be ready!
https://tamderudderjackson.com

@damo_danger_larkin – Another great sci-fi /fantasy writer from Dublin, Ireland. He has "danger" in his name, so you know it's going to be good! Plus, he's co-founder of the British & Irish Writing Community @bardoftheisles. He makes his debut in the book, too! Damien, see you in 2025 for the Gettysburg reunion!
https://www.damienlarkinbooks.com

@netts_shorts – An incredible short story writer that inspires me to be a better writer. She's the grand advocate for all indie authors with #indiefeaturefriday and just a dang good person. Nannette, thank you for your inspiration, and for not bragging when you kick my butt on Words with Friends.

https://linktr.ee/NannetteKreitzman

@thenixdamon - Her coming of age fiction book, *Moira*, is just one of her many talents. A lover of life and all things good, she has a soul that we should all aspire to. Nix, I'll be seeing you again, dear friend; hopefully in the great state of Texas!

@harpermcdavidauthor- My first Colorado book friend, who makes me smile with her clever wit. She wrote *Zapata*, a romance suspense novel that required her to change her name. Just saying. My kind of gal! Harper*, I enjoy our time together. You make me laugh.

https://www.harpermcdavid.com

These are just a few of the many. Go check out some new Indie writers, and for the love of God, leave them (us) a review.

Did you know when you leave a (great) review, it usually gets
featured in the next book and on my website?
Go to Goodreads or Amazon to post.

Print and digital books can be purchased on my website
or Amazon.

Follow for more information and insights:
www.michelepackard.com
Instagram: @aesopstories

Books by Packard
AESOP
FABLE
TELLER
COUNTERINTELLIGENCE
Scoochie-Scoochie Nite-Nite
Willed Ignorance - 2022

Life moves pretty fast.

Made in United States
Orlando, FL
09 January 2023